*What is Ducky running for . . . or from?*

Jamahl sidled over to Ducky. "I'm not afraid of Paula," he half-whispered. "I'll help you take down those campaign posters if you want me to."

After he said it, he ran on ahead into the house.

Ducky was surprised, but pleased. Jamahl was going to help her. She wasn't alone with her problem anymore.

She wasn't sure what she and Jamahl were going to do, but they'd have to do it secretly so Paula, her campaign manager, wouldn't know who had done it, and fast so Marybeth wouldn't find out Ducky had ever planned to run for president.

Otherwise she'd be like Arthur back there under the tree—a dead Ducky.

# RUN,
# DUCKY,
# RUN

# RUN, DUCKY, RUN

## LAEL LITTKE

Published by
Deseret Book Company
Salt Lake City, Utah

**Library of Congress Cataloging-in-Publication Data**

Littke, Lael.
     Run, Ducky, run / Lael Littke.
        p.    cm.—(Bee theres : bk. 6)
     "Cinnamon Tree."
     Summary: Ducky wants to be seventh-grade class president, but she fears that winning against another club member may cause her to lose her friends.
     ISBN 1-57345-134-7 (pbk.)
     [1. Schools—Fiction. 2. Clubs—Fiction. 3. Friendship—Fiction.] I. Title. II. Series.
PZ7.L719Ru    1996
[Fic]—dc20                              95-48820
                                                CIP
                                                AC

Printed in the United States of America

10  9  8  7  6  5  4  3  2  1

*For Eve, Gail, Martha, Elizabeth, Gloria,*
*Mary, Tony, Susan, and Mary Lou,*
*who are my Bee Theres*

# CHAPTER
1

Ducky found the poster when she was looking for a place to hide her diary.

Normally she didn't hide her diary. She knew her parents would never read it, and neither would her brother, Anton. He was sixteen. Twelve-year-old girls, Ducky included, were invisible to him.

But now that her cousin Dermott—or Demented, as Anton called him—was living with them, Ducky hid everything she didn't want him to see.

Dermott was nine. He was snoopy. He had something to say about everything Ducky did.

Not only that, but he said it loud. Real loud. He'd arrived at their house equipped with a microphone he'd received as a birthday gift, and he broadcast everything that went on. He wanted to grow up to be a TV newscaster and said he needed to practice.

1

Ducky didn't want him reading her diary at full volume to the whole neighborhood, the way he'd announced about her picture being in a current magazine. Not that there was anything she was ashamed of, either in the diary or in the magazine. The picture in the magazine was just part of an ad for shampoo. Sometimes Ducky modeled for ads and TV commercials. It was no big deal, and neither was her diary.

Actually, her diary was pretty dull, but still, a person didn't want everything she did yelled out to everybody within hearing distance. Especially right now, when she'd decided just yesterday to run for seventh-grade class president.

Last night she'd written in her diary about how Paula Powell at school had asked her to run for president. Paula had assured her that she was well enough known around school to win even though she was quite new in town. Being new was okay, Paula had said, because the seventh graders came from several different elementary schools and were *all* new to Woodward Junior High that year.

Ducky had never really thought about running for a school office, but she was flattered that Paula thought she could win. She'd written about that in the diary, too, and about how much she would like to win. She loved to be where the action was. She wouldn't want Dermott blatting all of that out through his mike.

The only safe place she could think of to hide her diary was behind the little door in her closet that led to a crawl space under the eaves of the house. It was when she opened the door and shone her flashlight inside that she saw the poster.

Somebody else had used this as a hiding place. But why hide a poster?

Pulling it out, she turned the flashlight on it. What she saw was a black-and-white photograph of the back of a girl's head. The girl had light-colored hair, cut short like girls wore in the old fifties movies Ducky sometimes watched on TV.

Above the photo, in large block letters, it said, "VOTE FOR:"

That was all. No name. Just "VOTE FOR:" and a picture of the back of a girl's head.

Ducky giggled to herself. It was a cool poster. Apparently the girl was well enough known that people would recognize even the back of her head.

It was a real coincidence for Ducky to find the poster right now, when she was running for president. Ducky's Aunt Aleesha, who claimed to be a conjure woman like one of their ancestors had been, would say that finding it was an omen.

But was it a good omen or a bad one?

If it was bad, Ducky could still call off running for president. Nobody knew yet that she was running, except Paula, who had insisted on being her campaign manager. Paula had said she would do everything that was necessary, including putting Ducky's picture up around campus and planning an introduction act for Monday, which was the day the campaigns started.

From downstairs Ducky heard the screech of Dermott's mike, which meant he'd just turned it on.

"Breakfast, everybody," Dermott boomed, shattering the peace of the Saturday morning. He liked to connect his mike with the CD system in the family room so he could get wall-shaking volume. "It's Uncle Walter's turn to cook breakfast," Dermott went on, "and that should make your stomach snap to attention. Look, folks, not one, not two, not three, but four different cereal boxes to choose from. Is that a feast, or what?"

Ducky heard a dull thud, which probably meant that Dad had pitched a cereal box at Dermott. Better still, maybe he'd pitched Dermott.

Maybe she should get Dermott to announce to her family her big news about running for class president.

Maybe she should even have him announce it to

the Bee Theres, which was a club made up of the members of her Beehive class.

The Bee Theres were having a meeting that very morning at McDonald's, their favorite eating place, before they spent the afternoon on service projects. If the meeting had been at her house, Ducky really would have had Dermott make her big announcement.

On the other hand, you never could trust Dermott to say only what you programmed him to say. She certainly wouldn't trust him at McDonald's. She dropped the whole idea.

Carefully placing her diary in the crawl space, Ducky closed the little door and stacked the boxes in front of it again. Then she picked up the poster showing the back of somebody's head and went downstairs.

Dad, Mom, Anton, and Dermott were already in the kitchen.

The table was set with pale green placemats and Mom's yellow-checked dishes. September sunlight coming through the window spotlighted the four cereal boxes that sat in the middle of the table, just as Dermott had announced.

Dermott zeroed in on the poster as soon as he saw it. "Whatcha got, Ducky?"

Ducky held it up. "I found it upstairs."

"Where upstairs?" Dermott's eyes lit up with curiosity.

"Never mind." Ducky turned the poster so everyone could see. "It's a real coincidence that I found it today, because I need to figure out how to make people vote for me."

She paused for a moment until everybody's eyes were on her. Then she said, "I've decided to run for president."

Dermott looked up from the poster and asked, "President of what?"

Anton, who'd been standing in front of the refrigerator, opened it. "Of the United States, Demented. What else?"

Ducky's dad was peeling apples at the sink. Glancing at the poster, he said, "Well, I'd give that girl credit for imagination. It must have attracted a lot of attention." Turning to Ducky he said, "I'm glad you're running, Ducky. It's a good thing to get involved in school politics."

Mom was pouring milk from a carton into her favorite white china pitcher. She liked to make the breakfast table look special on Saturday morning. "I think so too," she said. "I always knew you were the executive type, Marion. You'll be a terrific seventh-grade class president. Now sit down so we can eat."

Mom always called Ducky by her real name. She'd

been named after the great singer Marion Anderson, but she'd chosen the nickname Ducky so she wouldn't forget what it had felt like to be a tall, scrawny, bigfoot ugly duckling for so long, before everything suddenly seemed to fit together. She was going to be Marion again someday, after she'd done something that would make her worthy of the name.

Maybe she'd be a great seventh-grade president, like Mom said. If she was, maybe she'd call herself Marion afterwards.

Dermott wore a puzzled look. "Can girls be president?" he asked.

Anton was peering into the refrigerator now, his lanky frame bent almost double. Without turning around, he said, "If they can get people to vote for them they can." He took some orange juice from the refrigerator and drank straight from the carton.

"Anton!" Mom grabbed the carton and rubbed a dishcloth across where he'd had his mouth. "Can't you be an example for Dermott?"

"I *am* an example for Demented," Anton said cheerfully. "A ba-a-a-ad example." He put up a hand and Dermott gave him a high five. They both grinned.

Talk about demented. Both Anton and Dermott were demented.

Dermott turned on his mike. "Ducky for president, quack, quack, quack," he squawked.

Mom grabbed the mike and tucked it behind a geranium plant on the windowsill by the table. "I repeat, will everybody please sit down so we can eat!" There was a little frown line between her eyes, which meant they'd all better cool it because her EB was rising. That stood for Exasperation Barometer, something Anton had thought up.

Anton and Dermott sat.

Dad brought a bowl of sliced apples and bananas to the table. "A word of caution, Ducky," he said. "You've made a lot of progress in not being as impulsive as you used to be. I'm sure you'll think things through before you forge ahead with whatever you're going to do for your campaign."

Translated, that meant not to do anything that would embarrass him. He was the new principal at the junior high, and Ducky knew he wanted to maintain a certain image. He wouldn't be happy about her doing anything too absurd.

She held up the poster again. "This isn't too impulsive, is it? I mean, not this exactly, but something like it?" She remembered Dad's words about the poster girl. "Something with imagination?"

Dad smiled. "I'd say something like that is sure to catch everybody's attention."

"Ladies and gentlemen," Mom said. "Distinguished Candidate, Family Members, and Cousin Dermott. It is my pleasure to announce that breakfast is served. Let's get to it, okay?"

Dermott reached behind the geraniums for his mike. "I'll tell them, Aunt Monica," he said.

Mom grabbed the mike and put it in a high cupboard.

"Mom," Ducky said, "I'm not staying. The Bee Theres are having a meeting this morning. We're eating breakfast at McDonald's."

It was the wrong thing to say and the wrong time to say it. Mom took the poster from Ducky's hands and leaned it against the wall, then gently pushed her onto a chair. "All the more reason why you should put something nourishing into your stomach before you load up on grease and sugar." Mom sat down. "You know the rules, Marion. We eat breakfast together on Saturday morning."

They did have that rule. Mom was an office manager and left for work very early on weekday mornings, so breakfast was usually a do-it-yourself or sometimes a don't-do-it-at-all project. Saturdays were the best time to get everyone there at once.

It wasn't the time to argue. Sighing, Ducky reached for a cereal box and poured three Cheerios

9

out into her bowl. "I want to tell the Bee Theres I'm running for president," she said.

"It'll keep," Mom said shortly.

Dermott was watching Ducky. "Is she going to live in the White House?" he half-whispered to Anton.

"Sure," Anton half-whispered back. "If she wins."

Ducky opened her mouth to tell Anton to cool it, but Dad interrupted to ask Dermott to say the blessing on the food.

"Can I use my mike?" Dermott asked.

"In your dreams," Mom said, bowing her head.

Dermott muttered a few unintelligible phrases, then declared, "Amen."

Mom put a hand up to her ear. "What was that you said? Was it a blessing or your favorite rap?"

"If you'd let me use my mike, you'd know," Dermott said.

Mom put a hand to her forehead, which meant her EB had risen another couple of points.

Ducky sloshed milk onto her three Cheerios and downed them in a couple of swallows. She had to get out of there. Sometimes her family drove her crazy. Nobody, except Dermott, seemed to be interested about her running for class president.

The Bee Theres would care. They'd cheer and tell Ducky how exciting it was, and they'd probably insist on planning her campaign right then and there.

She stood up, announcing, "I have to go."

Mom threw her hands in the air. "Well, I tried. Don't blame me when you ruin your health by gulping hamburgers for breakfast."

Ducky hurried from the kitchen and headed for the front door, but just as she was going down the hallway, the telephone rang. She grabbed it. "Hello?"

"Paula Powell here," a firm voice said in her ear. "Just wanted to tell you I've got your campaign going."

"Already?" Ducky was surprised.

"Got a bunch of pictures printed up," Paula said. "Remember those shots Jamahl Picard snapped on the first day of school? There's a great one of you. On Monday you'll see your face on every tree and wall. Everybody will know who you are."

Ducky closed her eyes, imagining her face staring at her from every tree and wall on campus. It made her feel a little limp. But for sure people needed to know who she was before they could vote for her.

"Great," she said. "Thanks, Paula."

Paula said some other things, about how she'd had flyers printed up ready to distribute and how she'd turned in Ducky's name for the campaign assembly on Monday. Ducky had heard that she was called Powerhouse Paula, and now she began to understand why.

When Paula hung up, Ducky hurried out of the house.

The other Bee Theres were already at the Golden Arches when she got there. They all had big grins on their faces.

Becca, Carlie, Elena, Marybeth, and Sunshine giggled as she came up to the table.

Sunshine pulled out the sixth chair so Ducky could sit down. "We've got something great to tell you," she said.

"You'll never guess," Marybeth said. "It's really exciting."

"I've got something to tell you too," Ducky said. "But you tell first."

The others giggled again.

Marybeth's face absolutely glowed. "Ducky," she said, "I'm going to run for seventh-grade class president. I've always wanted to be president of something and now I'm going to try for it. I just turned in my name yesterday."

"And we're all going to be her campaign managers." Becca's glance took in all the Bee Theres, including Ducky. "We're going to make sure she's elected."

Marybeth nodded, smiling. "What do you think about that, Ducky?" she asked.

# CHAPTER
## 2

What did she think about that?

Ducky didn't think anything, because her brain was paralyzed with shock. Why hadn't somebody told her about Marybeth wanting to be president?

That was the trouble with being new in a group. You didn't know everything about the other people in it like you would if you'd been with them for a long time.

Feeling the eyes of the other Bee Theres on her, Ducky shaped her mouth into a smile. "Marybeth! How terrific!"

She hoped she sounded sincere. She *was* sincere. It *was* terrific that Marybeth was going to run, especially when she'd wanted to for so long.

But what was she, Ducky, going to do? She couldn't very well run against one of her new best friends,

13

could she? Especially when Paula had said she was sure to win.

Maybe Paula was just being nice. Maybe Ducky didn't really have a chance of winning.

But she'd always won whatever she had run for in her other school. She'd been voted Most Popular Student in the sixth grade. In fifth grade she'd been her class representative to the student council. Even in fourth grade she'd been elected to be the one from her grade to make a presentation about their school to the PTA.

Ducky collapsed onto the empty chair next to Marybeth, still airing her teeth in that big smile. "You'll be a great president, Marybeth," she said.

Marybeth held up both hands with her fingers crossed. "*If* I win I'll try to do my best."

"It'll be a landslide," Ducky assured her.

Marybeth grinned. "Don't I wish. We'll all go to the campus after our service projects to run off some flyers. And we have to plan my introduction act for Monday. It doesn't have to be any big deal. Just something to let everybody know who I am."

Ducky tried to keep smiling as Marybeth spoke. What was she going to do? She *liked* to be involved in things. She would enjoy being seventh-grade class president in this new school, if she won.

But was it worth hurting her new friend Marybeth by running against her?

No. It wasn't. She truly liked Marybeth and she loved being a member of the Bee Theres. She'd been very flattered to be invited *in.* Maybe they'd invite her *out* if she ran against Marybeth.

She made a decision. She would call Paula as soon as she got home and tell her to trash those posters. And the flyers. And all those plans Paula said she was cooking up, probably at that very moment.

Maybe she should call Paula *before* she got home. Maybe now.

She was opening her mouth to excuse herself to go find a phone when Becca said, "Well?"

Ducky looked at her, confused. "Well, what?"

"You said you had something to tell us too. So tell."

"Oh, that." Ducky had hoped they'd forgotten. "Not important," she said. "Not compared to Marybeth's news."

Sunshine put up a hand. "*I* know what it is." She looked triumphantly at Ducky.

Ducky felt limp. Keeping her candidacy a secret was like trying to carry water in a leaky bucket. Just when you plugged up one leak, another one started spurting. How had Sunshine found out? Had she been talking to Paula?

"Maybe now's not the time to tell it, Sunshine," she whispered.

"Sure it is." Sunshine held up a magazine, opened to the page with Ducky's picture in the shampoo ad. "Look at our famous friend. Think about it. This magazine goes all over the country, and our very own Ducky is in it."

"Wow." Carlie looked dazzled. "That's *great* news, Ducky."

Marybeth took the magazine and looked at the picture. "Your news is way better than mine, Ducky," she said.

Elena shoved a napkin across the table. "May I have your autograph, Celebrity?"

Ducky was so relieved that she almost melted off her chair. Sunshine didn't know her news after all.

"You're so famous," Becca said. "I remember seeing you in a commercial on TV before you ever moved into our ward. You know, the one where you have a bratty little brother and you're fighting over the last can of grapefruit juice in the fridge?"

"And you know what?" Ducky broke in, seeing a chance to change the subject. "Now that my cousin Dermott is staying with us, I really know what it's like to have a bratty little brother."

The others laughed.

"I can tell you more than you want to know about little brothers," Elena said.

Ducky knew that Elena had three little brothers.

Before they could ask if the magazine ad really was her big news, Ducky said, "Hey, did we come here to eat or to talk? I'm starved." Those three Cheerios she'd had at home hadn't done much for her.

Chair legs scraped against the floor as everybody got up.

"You guys get your McFood while I make a phone call," Ducky said. "I'll meet you at the table."

She hurried off toward the telephones, trying to remember the number Paula had given her.

Feeding some coins into the phone, she waited for it to ring. She felt a little sweaty. How was Paula going to take the news that all her efforts had been wasted?

After four rings Ducky was about to hang up, when somebody answered.

"H'lo?" It sounded like a kid. A boy.

"May I speak to Paula, please?" Ducky said.

"Who's this?"

"Tell her Ducky wants to speak with her, please."

The kid giggled. "She'll be mad if I say that."

"No, she won't. Why would she be mad?"

"She gets mad when she thinks I'm teasing her,"

the kid said. "If I tell her a ducky is calling, she'll smack me."

"I need to speak with her," Ducky insisted. "Don't tell her who's calling, then. Just say she's wanted on the phone."

"I can't," the kid said.

"Why not?" Ducky tried to be patient. This kid reminded her of Dermott.

"She's not here."

"Do you know when she'll be back?"

"She doesn't tell *me* stuff like that." His tone said that he was surprised she would even ask such a thing.

"Okay," Ducky said. "I'll call back later. Thanks."

Her heart was beating fast. What if Paula was out doing more things for Ducky's campaign? She wasn't called Powerhouse Paula for nothing. She might smack Ducky when she learned she wasn't running after all.

Well, there wasn't a whole lot Ducky could do about it at the moment. She couldn't go looking for Paula, since she had no idea where she was.

Ducky wished she'd told the Bee Theres right after Marybeth's announcement that she'd been asked to run for class president. She could have said right then that she'd decided not to run. If she'd said it then, maybe nobody would have thought much about it.

But it was too late to bring it up now. Wouldn't Marybeth be offended if she said now that she'd decided not to run? Marybeth would know she was pulling out because she thought she would win if she ran.

Or Marybeth might insist that she continue to run. Then, if what Paula said was true and she did win, Marybeth would be hurt.

Dad was always cautioning Ducky not to be too impulsive. But maybe she'd taken too long to think about things this time.

Well, she wasn't going to say anything at all. She would find Paula later and tell her the campaign was off. The Bee Theres would never know.

The other girls looked surprised when Ducky came to the table with just a small order of fries and a cup of water.

"Mom made me eat some cereal before I came," she said in explanation. Worrying had ruined her appetite.

Carlie, Elena, and Sunshine all had Egg McMuffins. Marybeth had a McChicken sandwich. Becca had a Big Mac. The Bee Theres never started a breakfast meeting before 10:30 in the morning, because that was the earliest McDonald's served Big

Macs, and Becca always had a Big Mac, morning, afternoon, or night.

"Maybe we should discuss our service projects," Marybeth said as everybody chewed.

Marybeth was their Beehive class president and conducted all their official class meetings.

"Let's not talk about them until we get to Sister Jackson's house," Sunshine said. "She'll have everything already planned." Sister Jackson was their Beehive teacher. She had asked the girls to save today for the service projects.

Becca put down her Big Mac. "Wasn't that why we were meeting here this morning? To plan the projects?"

Carlie shrugged. "That's as good an excuse as any. To tell the truth, I just wanted some junk food."

They all laughed together this time, as if they shared a secret. Ducky felt good, being part of such a fun group.

Would she still be part of it when they found out the secret she was keeping to herself?

# CHAPTER
## 3

After the Bee Theres finished eating, they started for Sister Jackson's house.

As they walked down Lake Avenue past the Buck-a-Cluck Chicken Shack, Sunshine stopped. "I want to see if Arvy's working today." Her cheeks turned pink as she said it.

Ducky knew that Sunshine liked Arvy Dixon. Her own face got a little warm because if Arvy was there, Jamahl Picard would be there too, and he was the one Ducky maybe liked. How can you tell for sure if you like somebody when he hasn't said more than five words to you since you met him?

Arvy and Jamahl had jobs at the Chicken Shack. They dressed up like big yellow chickens and passed out coupons for free samples of food.

That was how Jamahl was dressed when Ducky

first met him. You wouldn't think a guy dressed up like a chicken would make a big impression, but Ducky had liked the shy way he'd smiled at her when he'd taken his chicken head off. Sunshine had told her that Arvy called later to say that Jamahl thought Ducky was cute and wanted to know more about her.

She'd seen him at church each Sunday since then, but he'd never spoken to her. Just smiled shyly in her direction.

"I don't think they're here," Ducky said, looking all around the front of the Chicken Shack. She wished they were, because she was wearing her purple T-shirt with her neon pink vest over it. She knew those colors were good for her. Usually she had her hair done up in corn rows, but she had gotten tired of that and had undone all those little braids. Today she'd pulled her hair to the top of her head, fastened it with a rubber band, then let it cascade down. It was the way she'd worn it in one of the commercials she'd done, and she knew it looked good.

She would feel good about Jamahl seeing her that day.

Sunshine craned her neck to peer through the windows. "Let's go in and see if they're inside," she said.

"You and Ducky go in," Becca said. "You're the ones who like those big birds."

Ducky was a little embarrassed that they all guessed she liked Jamahl. But each of the Bee Theres had a certain guy she liked.

Sunshine grabbed her hand and pulled her toward the door. "We'll just say hello to them, like we were passing by and happened to think of them," she said.

Ducky let herself be dragged along.

There weren't very many people inside the Chicken Shack. Arvy and Jamahl for sure weren't there.

A tall guy behind the counter glanced at Ducky and Sunshine.

"You looking for the chickens?" he asked.

How did he know that?

"All the girls like those guys," he said, as if in explanation. "Maybe I should dress up like a chicken so girls would come looking for me." He grinned at them.

Ducky felt her face get warm again. It wasn't so much the guy's teasing them as it was the thought that other girls liked Jamahl. Other girls liked his shy smile as much as she did.

Did he talk to them?

Sunshine didn't look too happy either. "Let's go," she said. "We'll see them at church tomorrow."

Ducky was thinking about the campaign again. If

she ran for class president, Jamahl would *have* to notice her, wouldn't he?

He'd probably be totally impressed if he saw her picture all over campus the way Paula said it would be.

But she wasn't going to run, so what did it matter? She wasn't going to risk losing her best friends.

The other Bee Theres giggled when Sunshine and Ducky got back out to the sidewalk. Becca put her hands in her armpits to make wings of her arms and strutted around saying, "Puck-puck-puck-puck-puck, I know who likes that cluck-cluck-cluck-cluck-cluck."

Sunshine and Ducky laughed with the others. It was so much fun to have good friends to share things with.

Sister Jackson was waiting for them when they got to her house. She had six little baskets lined up on the kitchen table, ready to be filled with chocolate chip cookies, she said, to take to people for the girls' service projects.

"We'll make the cookies," she said, "and I'll drive you around to deliver them. We'll make a few extra for ourselves."

Elena cheered. "Wait till you sink your teeth into

one of Sister Jackson's cookies," she told Ducky. "We call them Perfection Confections."

It seemed to Ducky that Sister Jackson did everything to perfection. Her house looked perfect, like a model home that you might see in a new housing development. Her clothes were always neat and coordinated. Her hair seemed to be starched—there was never a single strand out of place. Even her teeth were straight and white and perfect.

The other girls had told Ducky that when Sister Jackson first became their teacher, they had tried to get rid of her because she wanted them to do everything perfectly. But they liked her now.

Their first teacher, Pamela, hadn't worried about perfection. Pamela was beautiful and glamorous and took them on shopping trips to the mall and had sleepovers at her apartment. She was an airline attendant and had quit being their teacher when she went home to Idaho to get ready for her wedding. When she'd come back to get married, the whole Beehive class had been bridesmaids, including Ducky, whose family had just moved to town. It had been one of the most fun things Ducky had ever done.

Maybe perfect Sister Jackson could help her find a perfect way to tell Paula that she wasn't running for president. Maybe she could think up a way to keep everybody happy.

But Ducky didn't have a chance to ask her. As soon as the cookies were baked and cooled, the girls packed them up in the little baskets and carried them to Sister Jackson's car.

Carlie sighed as she finished the last of the cookies they'd made for themselves. "Someday," she said, "I want to have a party where all we do is sit around and eat chocolate chip cookies for about four hours."

"Me too," Elena said. "But what I want is to not bake them. Just eat the dough. That's my favorite thing."

"Me too," the others echoed.

Sister Jackson settled in behind the steering wheel. "That's a little dangerous. You can get salmonella from eating raw eggs."

Everybody groaned.

"Tell you what I'll do," she said. "I'll adjust my recipe for Perfection Confections so that I can use those frozen egg substitutes. Then the next time we have a good reason for a celebration, we'll have cookie dough for refreshments."

"We'll celebrate when Marybeth wins the election," Becca said.

Sister Jackson asked what election they meant, and they talked about how Marybeth was running for seventh-grade class president all the way to their first stop, which was at the home of the person Ducky was to visit for her service project.

"Her name is Sister Truesdale," Sister Jackson said as they stopped in front of the house. "You'll like her, Ducky. She recently moved here from Wyoming because she has a health problem and needs to live in a warm climate. She bought a house in an area zoned for animals since she said she couldn't leave them behind."

Ducky could have guessed that. Sister Truesdale had a small house set in the middle of a big yard. There were lots of trees, and it seemed as if a different kind of animal had taken up residence under each one of them. She could see some ducks inside a low, fenced enclosure that contained what looked like a child's wading pool. Dogs roamed freely around the shaded lawn. There were cats perched on the porch railing. And a goat came to peer through the wrought-iron gate at her as she got out of the car.

"Ba-a-a-a-ah," he said, watching her.

"Sister Truesdale is expecting you, Ducky," Sister Jackson said. "I called and told her she was going to have a lovely visitor."

Ducky hoped Sister Jackson hadn't built her up too much. She wouldn't want to disappoint Sister Truesdale.

"Carlie's service project is close by, and so is

Becca's," Sister Jackson said. "We'll go deliver their cookies while you get acquainted." She started to drive away, then stopped and poked her head out of the window. "Don't worry about the goat," she said. "He's friendly."

Ducky hoped so. He came right up to her when she opened the gate and began nibbling the ribbons on the little basket she carried. When she lifted it out of his reach, he chewed on the bottom edge of her T-shirt instead.

She tried to shoo the goat away as she rang the doorbell, but he got a good tooth-hold on her T-shirt and went right on munching.

She stood there waiting, one arm holding the basket high and the other flapping at the goat. That's the way she was when the door opened and she saw Jamahl Picard standing there.

He stared at her as if he didn't know what to say.

Arvy Dixon stood behind him, looking over his shoulder.

"Hi, Ducky," he said. "We were just talking about you. Did you know your picture is hanging up all over school?"

# CHAPTER
# 4

Was she in a nightmare or something? Was she really standing there at a stranger's front door with one arm held high like the Statue of Liberty while a goat nibbled at her shirt and Jamahl Picard stared blankly at her through the screen door?

Had Arvy Dixon really just announced that her picture was already hanging up all over the campus?

She wished she could reshoot this scene the way the commercials people sometimes reshot a scene that didn't work right. This was supposed to be a service project, with just her and Sister Truesdale as the characters. The way it was supposed to play was that Sister Truesdale came to the door and accepted the basket of cookies while saying something about how Beehive girls were the best you could find when it came to service projects.

But there was no reshooting this scene.

Ducky didn't know what her lines were supposed to be.

Jamahl didn't say anything. Maybe he didn't know *his* lines either. He just stood there grinning shyly as he opened the screen door.

The goat followed Ducky inside. He seemed to be permanently attached to her T-shirt.

"Have you been to the campus?" Arvy asked.

Silently Ducky shook her head.

"There are posters with your picture on every wall and every tree." Arvy repeated what he'd already told her.

She didn't think she could speak. How had Paula gotten the posters hung up so fast? The other Bee Theres wouldn't be passing the campus and see them, would they?

No, they weren't going in that direction.

They'd be going there later to run off Marybeth's flyers. But by then Ducky would have found Paula and gotten her to take the posters down.

Right now she had to be nice to Sister Truesdale.

The room Ducky entered was cheerful, filled with sunshine and animals. Ducky counted three cats perched on windowsills and the backs of chairs. A brown dog regarded her from a doorway. He didn't bark.

Ducky looked around, still holding the cookie basket up out of the goat's reach. Was she in the right house? Where *was* this Sister Truesdale she had come to visit?

She asked the question aloud. "Where is Sister Truesdale?"

"She's looking for Arthur," Arvy said. "He's dead, you know. We're going to bury him in the backyard." He pointed toward the back of the house with a small shovel he carried. "She said he was here this morning, but she can't find him now. She said maybe somebody ate him."

Jamahl's shy smile faded and he looked mournful.

This *had* to be a nightmare. Ducky wondered if she should just put the cookies down somewhere and run.

"Who is Arthur?" she asked. Her voice sounded hollow in her own ears. Why hadn't somebody said something about a death in the family?

Before the boys could answer, a tall woman came through an arched doorway that led to a hall. She was skinny as a mop handle and had a bush of red hair, which made her look even more like a mop.

"I found Arthur," she said. "I remember now that I put him in a closet this morning away from Gruff and the cats. Gruff will eat anything." She stopped when she saw Ducky. "Oh, my dear," she said, "you must be Ducky Dumont. I'm Estelle Truesdale. Rhoda Jackson said you were coming by this morning."

She came over and smoothly took the basket of cookies from Ducky's high-held hand. "Well now, isn't this nice? We'll have refreshments after the funeral. Thank you." With her other hand she grasped Ducky's hand and squeezed it. "Do you have time to join us in saying good-bye to Arthur?" she asked.

Ducky didn't know how long Sister Jackson and the other girls would be gone. Maybe they were out in front right now, waiting for her. She hoped so.

"I don't know," she said. She turned to look back out through the front door.

The goat, still attached, turned with her.

Sister Truesdale seemed to notice him for the first time.

"Gruff!" she said. "Bad boy." She flapped her hand at the goat. For the first time since Ducky had opened the front gate, he stopped nibbling her shirt.

"His name is Gruff," Sister Truesdale explained. "You know, like in the Three Billy Goats Gruff?"

The goat stood gazing at Ducky with his odd eyes. They had oval pupils instead of round.

"You'll have to forgive Gruff," Sister Truesdale said. "He has no manners."

This was a madhouse. But at least now Ducky knew who Gruff was. But who was Arthur? And why were they burying him in the backyard?

"I have to go," she said.

"Stop by the campus," Arvy said, "and see all those posters about you running for president. The pictures are copies of one Jamahl took last week."

Jamahl looked proud.

Ducky had almost forgotten about the posters, what with all the talk of funerals and stuff. What was she going to do about them? She had to do something before Marybeth and the other girls saw them.

Sister Truesdale smiled. "Isn't that nice that you're running for president? Rhoda Jackson said you're new in town, and here you are so popular already."

Ducky scarcely heard her. She was thinking of sneaking over to the campus and gathering up all those posters. Maybe she could drop them into Arthur's grave when they had his funeral.

"How soon are you having Arthur's funeral?" she asked.

"Right now," Sister Truesdale said. "Arvy, will you go finish digging the grave? And Jamahl, you help me get him laid out in his coffin."

Arvy headed for the back door. "The grave will be ready in five minutes," he said. "I dug part of it before

33

me and Jamahl came in for a drink." He turned to go out.

Oh, no. Things were going too fast. Ducky felt her heart race.

"Listen, you guys," she said desperately. "You know those posters you saw?"

Arvy and Jamahl nodded.

"It's kind of, y'know, embarrassing to have your face hung on every wall and tree. How'd you like to help me gather them all up and we'll bury them with Arthur?"

Arvy shook his head. "Huh-UH! Not me. The Dragon would kill me if I messed her up."

"Dragon?" Ducky was puzzled. Was he talking about Sister Truesdale?

"Yeah," Arvy said. "Paula the Dragon. She's the one who put up those posters. Nobody messes with Paula unless they want to get scorched. Are you friends with her?"

"Sort of," Ducky said. This was getting worse and worse. Was Paula going to scorch her when she said she wasn't going to run after all?

"Is there a problem, Ducky?" Sister Truesdale was watching her with sharp blue eyes.

Ducky wondered how much she could tell her. It would be nice to tell *somebody*.

But not in front of Arvy and Jamahl.

"I don't know," she said. "Maybe not."

Maybe not, if she could just keep Marybeth and the others away from the campus until she talked to Paula.

"May I use your telephone?" she asked.

"Of course you may, Ducky," Sister Truesdale said. "As soon as you're finished, come out in the backyard and help us sing over Arthur's grave."

She pointed to a nook in the hall where the telephone was; then she and the boys disappeared.

Gruff followed Ducky as she went to the phone and punched in Paula's number again. He nibbled gently at her jeans as she counted the rings. One, two, three, four. There was a click and an answering machine came on. The voice sounded like the kid she'd spoken to earlier.

"If you want to talk to Dad or Mom," the voice on the machine said, "leave a message after the beep. If you're a girl and want Dave, take a number and get in line. If you want to talk to Carson, leave a message in the hole in the old sycamore tree in front of my house. If you want to talk to Paula, think twice about it and hang up."

Ducky hung up.

Maybe she didn't want to talk to Paula. Maybe it would be safer just to go ahead and run in the campaign.

But how would she tell Marybeth?

Following the sound of voices, Ducky went out through the back door to the big backyard. Gruff followed her, bleating softly. He seemed to have fallen in love with her, which pleased Ducky, in a way. It was nice to have somebody like you when your world was falling apart, even if it was only a goat.

Sister Truesdale, Arvy, and Jamahl were standing by a hole that had been dug under a spreading oak tree. A shoebox with a wide blue ribbon around it lay beside the hole. Jamahl was on his knees writing on a tombstone-shaped piece of cardboard with a Magic Marker. "Here lies Arthur," he wrote.

The shoebox must be the coffin. Ducky was relieved. She hadn't really thought Arthur was a person, but things had been so weird today that she wouldn't have been too surprised if he was.

As she walked closer, she saw that there were two other cardboard tombstones under the tree. One said "Mitzi" on it. Another said "Wilmer."

"We're going to sing 'Whispering Hope,'" Sister Truesdale said. "Do you know that song, Ducky?"

Ducky nodded. Sometimes, when her mom could get Anton to cooperate, her whole family sang around the piano, and that was one of the songs her dad liked.

Sister Truesdale hummed a note, then started to sing: "Soft as the voice of an angel . . ."

Arvy and Jamahl joined in. It was the first time Ducky had heard Jamahl's voice that day. He sang the melody along with Sister Truesdale, in a high, clear tenor. Arvy sang the harmony, and Ducky joined in with him.

Gruff stood in front of Ducky, gazing up at her as she sang. It was pretty, the music there under the tree in the bright morning sunshine.

When they finished, Ducky asked, "Was Arthur a cat?"

"No," Sister Truesdale said. "He was a duck."

After Arvy put the shoebox into the hole and filled in the grave with the small shovel, they all headed for the house.

Jamahl sidled over to Ducky. "I'm not afraid of Paula," he half-whispered. "I'll help you take down those posters if you want me to."

After he said it, he ran on ahead into the house.

Ducky was surprised, but pleased. Jamahl was going to help her. She wasn't alone with her problem anymore.

She wasn't sure what she and Jamahl were going to do, but they'd have to do it secretly so Paula wouldn't know who had done it, and fast so Marybeth wouldn't find out Ducky had ever planned to run for president.

Otherwise she'd be like Arthur back there under the tree—a dead Ducky.

# CHAPTER
## 5

"I guess Jamahl and I better go," Arvy said as they all walked back toward the house, "now that we've got Arthur buried."

Sister Truesdale opened the screen door. "Don't you want to have something to eat? Seems like everybody always eats after a funeral. I wonder why that is. Maybe just to prove we're still alive."

Nobody offered any different explanation, but Arvy asked, "What would we eat?"

Sister Truesdale held the screen door open as Arvy, Ducky, and Jamahl went inside. She tried to close it before Gruff could invite himself in too, but he stuck his head inside before the door could shut, then inched in the rest of the way. He planted himself in front of Ducky, gazing adoringly at her the way he had done out by the grave.

Sister Truesdale closed the door. "Ducky brought those cookies," she said. "I can rustle up some Kool-Aid."

Arvy looked interested. "You in a hurry?" he asked Jamahl.

"No." Jamahl shook his head. "Unless Ducky wants to do something with those posters real quick." He flicked a glance at Ducky, then looked shyly away.

Ducky had never known anybody as shy as he was. She didn't know very many shy people. The men and women she worked with on commercials and ads were anything but shy. Nobody would ever call her family shy either. Dad always spoke as if he expected to be obeyed, and Mom was used to bossing people around. Anton? Forget it. He didn't know the meaning of shy. And Dermott? The less said about him the better.

As for herself, she had lacked confidence back in those days when she'd been an ugly duckling, but she'd never been shy.

Jamahl's shyness made Ducky want to treat him gently, like a skittish deer that would flee if you scared it.

"I'm not in that much of a hurry," she said. She really was, since she wanted to get rid of those posters before Marybeth and the other Bee Theres had a chance to see them. But she had to wait for Sister Jackson to come back and pick her up, didn't she?

"I have to wait for Sister Jackson to come back," she said aloud.

If she did that, though, maybe Marybeth would ask Sister Jackson to drop all the girls off at the campus so they could do her flyers. Then how would Ducky explain why her face looked at them from every wall and tree?

"Jamahl could give you a ride on his bike," Arvy suggested.

Jamahl looked ready to run away. Ducky couldn't imagine him letting her share his bike, his arms around her as she perched on the crossbars, his breath in her hair as they rode along.

And she couldn't imagine what she would say when the Bee Theres arrived on campus.

Moreover, she couldn't imagine how she was going to explain to Paula why the posters were not there on Monday morning.

But she *had* to get rid of them, and soon. She would just have to do it and think of the consequences later.

Gruff took a step forward and nuzzled her hand, covering it with soft goat kisses and nibbling at her thumb.

Ducky looked down at him. Maybe she and

Jamahl could take the goat along and let him loose there with the posters. Sister Truesdale said he ate everything. They could blame him for the destruction of the pictures.

But animals were forbidden on campus. There would be questions as to how Gruff had gotten there, and maybe Sister Truesdale would get into trouble.

"I can walk," Ducky said. "I really would like to go to the campus as soon as possible."

She was aware that Sister Truesdale was watching her closely.

"*I'll* walk," Jamahl said gallantly. "You ride."

Ducky turned to Sister Truesdale. "Will you tell Sister Jackson and the other girls that I had to go because I have to . . ." What explanation could she offer for running off before they came back? "Tell them something really important came up and I have to do something as soon as possible and that—"

Sister Truesdale put up a hand. "Back in Wyoming we used to say, 'The least said, the sooner mended.' I'll just say you had to go." She dragged her lovesick goat away from Ducky's jeans, which he'd begun to nibble again. "Come back when you can and we'll talk about it."

Ducky felt her face grow warm. Sister Truesdale

didn't think she was doing anything *wrong*, did she? Because she wasn't. Was she?

Wouldn't it be easier if she just waited for the other girls and *told* them she'd planned to run for class president?

But why should she do that when she was so close now to destroying the evidence and calling the whole thing off?

Would Dad say she was being impulsive again?

Ducky squashed that thought.

"Have a cookie and some Kool-Aid," she said to Jamahl. "Then we'll go."

Ducky felt guilty about riding the bike and having Jamahl jog alongside, especially when he was full of cookies and Kool-Aid. So she walked too, and he pushed the bike. They didn't say much as they hurried along the sidewalk. Jamahl didn't seem to have much to say, and Ducky was so worried about the other girls getting to the campus ahead of them that she couldn't hold a conversation.

Besides, they were using all their breath to cover the two miles to the campus in the least possible time.

They were both puffing as they arrived in front of the odd-colored junior high building. Becca called it barf-tan, but Elena always said it wasn't that bad.

What was bad right now was that, just as Jamahl

and Arvy had said, Ducky's face grinned out from every spot where a poster could be hung. VOTE FOR DUCKY, the posters demanded in big print.

Marybeth would have a cow if she saw all that.

"Let's start with the ones on the trees," Ducky said to Jamahl. "They're the first ones people see."

Without asking questions, Jamahl laid down his bike and went to the closest poster.

*"Hey!"* somebody roared as he began to pull out the tack that held it to the tree.

It was Paula. She came sweeping around the corner of the building like a high wind and gusted toward Jamahl. "You touch that poster, Jamahl Picard, and you're dog meat," she yelled.

Jamahl backed away from the tree.

"I'll have you expelled for unfair tactics," Paula blustered, coming to slap a protective hand on the poster. "Are you working for Eddie Howland or something? This is the kind of thing I'd expect from *his* friends."

Ducky remembered that Paula had told her Eddie Howland was running for president too, and also Chester Burkey. But she'd said that Ducky (with Paula's help) could easily leave them both in the dust.

Jamahl straightened up. "I, I, I . . ."

Ducky couldn't let him take the blame for this. "Paula," she began.

Paula turned on her. "Oh, Ducky," she said, suddenly a gentle breeze compared to the tornado she'd just been. "Don't you love what I've done? And I just finished running off a whole pile of flyers and stacked them outside every classroom in the school."

Ducky felt weak. "Paula," she said again. "Paula, I . . ." She sounded just like Jamahl.

"I know you're overcome," Paula said. "I think it's pretty terrific too. We're going to win this campaign, Ducky Dumont. Then we'll turn this place around, all right."

What was she talking about? They hadn't even discussed what things Ducky would try to do if she won. Did Paula expect to run things if Ducky became president?

"Paula," Ducky said once again. "I . . ."

Once again Paula interrupted. "You just stick with me, Ducky, and we'll totally wipe out the opposition. I've got some Power Ranger costumes that we'll use in your introduction on Monday and when you explain your platform on Tuesday. We'll show everybody just exactly how we plan to operate." She glanced at her watch. "I gotta dash."

"Wait," Ducky said. She felt like she was being

steamrollered. This was *her* campaign, and she didn't think she wanted the Power Ranger image.

"I want to handle my own intro act," she said. "And the speech on Tuesday. I'll take care of that, too."

Thunderclouds began to gather on Paula's face again. But then she smiled. "Okay. But I'll be ready to step in if things don't work out."

She sounded as if she knew things wouldn't work out.

Looking at her watch again, she said, "Now I do have to go." She turned to Jamahl. "If these posters are gone on Monday, Jamahl, guess who's going to be scraping his nose off the sidewalk." She hurried away after throwing him a final glare.

Ducky and Jamahl silently watched her go.

"There's been a change in plans," Ducky said when Paula turned down a side street.

"Yeah," Jamahl breathed. "I'm scared of her."

He didn't even sound embarrassed about being afraid of a girl. But Paula was no ordinary girl.

"I should have told her I wasn't going to run after all," Ducky said.

Jamahl looked at her with disbelief. "She'd have loosened all your teeth."

Dismally, Ducky silently agreed with him.

"What am I going to do now?" she asked aloud.

"Marybeth and the others are going to be here any minute." She wished she'd been as clever as that girl whose poster she'd found in the crawl space at her house that morning. She wished she'd had a picture of the back of her head put on the posters. With no name. People wouldn't have recognized her, and she'd have had a little more time to think about what she could do so Marybeth wouldn't be hurt.

But maybe she could do something else weird. Was there some way she could disguise all these posters?

"Jamahl," she said, "do you still have that Magic Marker you were using to make Arthur's tombstone?"

Jamahl nodded. Pulling two pens from his pocket, he held them out toward her.

"Let's do a little changing on my face." Without letting herself think of what Paula would say, Ducky took one of the thick pens and drew a duck bill on the nearest picture.

Jamahl looked puzzled.

"I don't want anybody to vote for me," Ducky explained as she drew. "So I want to make myself look real flaky."

Jamahl didn't ask questions. With the other marker, he began drawing a duck bill on another picture.

46

"Somebody's going to get in trouble for this," he said. But he kept on drawing.

"I'll sign my name to each one." Ducky scribbled her name across the duck-billed face on the poster in front of her. "That way people will know I did it."

"Maybe," Jamahl murmured. He look worried, but he hurried on to the next poster.

It wasn't until they'd done at least twenty of them that Ducky remembered Paula had said she'd put flyers outside all the classroom doors.

This campaign was already out of control. And worse still, Ducky spotted Sister Jackson's car stopping in front of the barf-colored school building. Marybeth, along with Becca, Carlie, Elena, and Sunshine, got out and stared at the altered pictures of Ducky.

It was too late to hide.

Ducky put the cap back on the thick felt pen, shoved it into her jeans pocket, and started to walk toward her friends.

# CHAPTER
# 6

Marybeth was the first to speak.

"Ducky," she said, "what are you doing here?" Her eyes went from Ducky to Jamahl, back to Ducky, then to the disfigured posters.

"Vote for Ducky," she read.

"Sister Truesdale said you had something important to do," Becca said. "Is this it?" She looked at the nearest poster, squinting a little as if it hurt her eyes.

"Is this the news you couldn't tell us?" Sunshine asked. "You're running for president?"

Ducky thought of a hymn the choir had sung in church the previous Sunday. It started out, "If you could hie to Kolob in the twinkling of an eye." If she'd had the choice at that moment of either standing there trying to answer the question or hieing anywhere—Kolob, Pluto, even Pomona—in the twinkling of an eye, she wouldn't have hesitated about choosing to hie, whatever that meant.

She managed a small laugh, more like one of Gruff's bleats. "Caught red-handed," she blurted, not able to think of anything else to say.

She was aware that Jamahl had come to stand by her side. He didn't say anything, but Jamahl suddenly seemed like a tower of bashful strength.

"It was going to be a surprise," Ducky blundered on, wondering what she could say next.

"It's a surprise, all right," Sunshine and Carlie said together.

Marybeth didn't say anything.

Becca was looking at Ducky, her eyes narrowed again. "Why didn't you tell us back at McDonald's that you were running for president?"

Ducky's face felt hot. "I didn't want to take anything away from Marybeth's announcement," she said, which was the truth.

There was an awkward moment of silence. Then Marybeth stepped forward and put an arm around Ducky's waist. "Well, hey, this is great. No matter which one of us wins, a Bee There will be leading the seventh grade."

Ducky returned her hug. "Maybe not. Paula said Eddie Howland is running too. And Chester Burkey."

"Paula?" Becca grabbed the name as if it were a

basketball she was going to run with. "You're working with Paula the Pirate?"

She exchanged a look with the other girls.

Powerhouse Paula? Paula the Dragon? Now Paula the Pirate? How many nicknames did Paula have?

Ducky wondered again if she'd made a mistake going along with Paula, but before she could ask, Carlie said, "Either one of you can beat Eddie Howland. He runs for everything but never wins. Don't worry about Eddie. Chester either," she added as an afterthought.

Ducky still had an arm around Marybeth's waist. "Well, I'll never win against you," she said, "so Jamahl and I were just going to have fun with the campaign. You know, really goof it up." She waved a hand at the redecorated pictures of herself. "Everybody will vote for you because they know you. I'm new, so it doesn't matter what kind of stupid stuff I do."

"Don't be too sure that I'll win," Marybeth said. "Everybody has seen you in ads and commercials so they know who you are, and they all like you, even though you're new."

Miserably, Ducky realized that was true. Kids *did* like her. She'd never even considered that being popular could be a problem.

But Marybeth was popular too, wasn't she? She

would make a great president, and she really wanted to do it. She *should* be president.

Ducky made a decision. She was going to stay in the campaign, but she was going to make sure she lost the election.

Making her eyes go slightly out of focus, she put her index fingers to her temples and lowered her voice to a hoarse croak. "The famous psychic Madame Ducky Dumont predicts that the winner of this election will be . . ." She paused dramatically, then pointed both hands toward Marybeth. ". . . will be *Marybeth*," she declared. "Madame Ducky is always right."

All of the girls laughed then, and the tension seemed to be broken.

"You know what?" Elena said. "This is a great opportunity to show kids how a campaign should be run. I mean, you won't be saying bad things about each other, and you can be good friends throughout the whole thing, no matter who wins."

"Tell that to Paula," Sunshine commented.

Carlie and Becca groaned.

Ducky felt nervous again. There were undercurrents here at school that she hadn't even been aware of. "Tell me about Paula," she urged.

"Forget Paula," Marybeth said. "You're right,

Elena. This will be a great chance to put on a campaign that everybody will remember."

Ducky hoped they would remember it for the right reasons.

After Marybeth, Elena, Becca, Carlie, and Sunshine went in to run off the flyers for Marybeth, Ducky and Jamahl finished drawing duck bills on all the pictures of Ducky they could find. Across each one she signed her name.

"Tell me about Paula," Ducky said again as they worked.

Jamahl seemed reluctant to say anything. "Maybe she's not as bad as everybody thinks," he finally said.

That didn't seem like much comfort.

"What's she going to say when she sees what we've done with these?" Ducky stepped back to look at the duck bill she'd just drawn. Had she been too impulsive about ruining the posters?

Jamahl continued to draw. "Yell and stomp, most likely," he said. "Whack off a few heads, mine included."

Ducky was shocked. "Why are you helping me then, if you're so afraid of her?"

Jamahl didn't look at her. "Because you asked me to."

He might be shy, but he certainly wasn't wimpy, even though he was terrified of Paula.

"Would you like to walk home with me?" Ducky asked. "Maybe we can make some plans. I told Paula I'd handle my own introduction on Monday and my speech on Tuesday."

"I know," Jamahl said, putting the final touches on a bill and shoving the felt pen into his pocket. "Sure, I'd like to walk home with you."

As they walked toward her house, Ducky told Jamahl about how she'd just decided she was going to make sure she lost the election.

He glanced at her and said, "That's going to be hard."

"I want you to help me lose," she said.

He was silent for a moment. "If that's what you want." He kicked a rock that was in the middle of the sidewalk. "What would you like me to do?"

She thought about it. "Well, we could plan something totally dumb for my introduction on Monday, something that will really trash me. Do you have any ideas?"

He stared at his feet as they walked a dozen paces. Then he looked up and said, "Maybe."

"What?"

"*What* what?"

"What ideas?"

He grinned. "Maybe I shouldn't tell you."

Ducky stopped and put her hands on her hips.

"Jamahl Picard," she said, "you aren't going to make me look *too* foolish, are you?"

He looked at her, his eyebrows raised. "Who, me?" he said.

Ducky decided right then and there that she could get a great big crush on him if she wasn't careful. And he seemed to like her too.

Dermott almost ended that before it even got started.

Ducky should have realized before taking Jamahl home that Dermott would have his mike hooked up, as usual, and would be eager to use it.

He must have been standing at the door watching the street, because as soon as Ducky and Jamahl came in sight of the house he began telling the whole neighborhood.

"Well, look at this," he announced. "Can you believe it? Ducky's found a boyfriend. She's bringing him home for everybody to see, so take a good look, folks, before he gets away. Ducky's got a guy-guy-guy-guy-guy."

He must have turned the volume up full blast, because the last word echoed all over the neighborhood.

Ducky glanced at Jamahl, hoping he'd suddenly gone temporarily deaf.

He was looking with interest toward Ducky's house. "You got a little brother?" he asked.

"Cousin," she confessed. "He's pretty obnoxious."

Jamahl grinned.

Ducky considered telling him how it was with Dermott, how his dad was dead and his mother had just up and dropped him off at their house one day. His life hadn't been easy.

But that didn't make him any less obnoxious.

"Hey," Ducky said. "Maybe we could use him. I mean, Dermott could lose an election for *anybody*."

Jamahl nodded. "Let's talk to him."

Ducky put her hands over her ears to keep out Dermott's announcements about how she'd never brought a guy-guy-guy home before.

When they got to the porch, Jamahl walked up the stairs and gently took the mike from Dermott.

"Cool it, dude," he said. "We want to talk to you."

"Yeah?" Dermott looked suspicious. "What about?" He reached for his mike, but Jamahl put it behind his back.

"About my running for class president," Ducky said. "Want to help us with something?"

"No," Dermott said.

Ducky felt like kicking herself. She should have known that wasn't the way to approach Dermott.

Jamahl must have known too, because he leaned over and whispered something into Dermott's ear.

Dermott's eyes widened. He grinned, showing all those teeth that seemed too big for his mouth.

"Yeah," he said. "I'd like that." His eyes shifted to Ducky. "Does she know?" he asked out of the side of his mouth.

"Not everything," Jamahl whispered back.

Dermott turned toward the door. "I'm gonna get Anton," he said. "He'll want to help."

Opening the door, he ran inside, yelling, "Anton! Anton!"

As soon as he was out of sight, Ducky said, "What did you tell him? I thought we were going to have to resort to bribery."

Jamahl shrugged. "I was a bratty little brother once too. I just asked him if he wouldn't like to help trash you. That's all it took."

That figured. No wonder Dermott wanted to get Anton in on it.

Ducky hoped she wouldn't regret letting Anton and Dermott in on her trashing.

# CHAPTER
7

Anton was only too willing to assist. He clattered down the stairs behind Dermott, grinning.

"What exactly do I get to do?" he asked.

He might have inquired first as to *why* they were going to trash Ducky. He might have given her a chance to tell him about wanting to lose the election and the reason behind it. He might have been a little less happy about the idea.

"Guys!" Ducky said disgustedly.

Anton raised his eyebrows in fake bewilderment. "What's the problem? We're doing what you want, aren't we?" He turned to Jamahl. "Aren't we?"

"Look," Jamahl said, "we haven't got much time to plan this. We've got to get our artillery pulled together if we're going to shoot her down."

Ducky appreciated that Jamahl was trying to get

things going. But he could have said it another way. He could have made some explanation to Anton to show that he liked her and was only doing this because she had asked him to.

Ducky wasn't happy with any of the three of them. Would any of them have been this willing to cooperate if she'd wanted to *win* the election?

Planting her hands on her hips, she glared at Anton. "Aren't you even going to ask the reason behind all this?"

Anton put a hand on his chest, and Ducky knew he was going to quote from one of the crummy poems he liked to memorize.

With a corny, sad gaze upward, he said, "'Ours not to reason why; ours but to do or die.'"

Dermott looked alarmed. "Die? Nobody said nothing to me about dying."

"*Anything*," Ducky corrected. "Nobody said *anything* to me about dying."

"Me neither," Dermott agreed, nodding vigorously.

Ducky threw up her hands in exasperation. They were all hopeless.

"Jamahl says he has some ideas," Ducky told her brother and her cousin.

"I do," Jamahl agreed. "Do you have any construction paper? Or just plain stiff paper? Cardboard, maybe? And some paints of some kind?"

"What do you want that kind of stuff for?" Dermott asked.

Jamahl looked slyly at Ducky. "It's going to be a surprise," he said.

The guys didn't tell Ducky what they were planning. Anton said it wasn't necessary for her to know. He said sometimes the introduction of a candidate came off better if there was an element of surprise, even for the candidate himself.

"Or *her*self," he added before Ducky could correct him.

She had misgivings about letting them have a free hand with this. But they were not going to tell her anything. And, after all, she wanted to make a *bad* impression, as far as being a candidate was concerned.

Maybe not as bad as what they were cooking up, though.

She was especially suspicious when the three of them left the house, saying they were going to Jamahl's since they needed some equipment he had there.

She let them go and went upstairs to write in her

diary. Pulling it out from behind the little door in the closet, she sat down at her desk and picked up a pen.

"Paula says I'm a sure winner," she began writing. "I'd kind of like to be president, but the trouble is, Marybeth really wants the job. She'd probably hate me if I won, and so would the other Bee Theres."

Chewing on the end of the pen, she gazed at the poster of the back of a girl's head. She could sympathize with that girl. She was going into a campaign backwards too.

Putting her pen to paper again, she wrote, "I'd rather be one of the Bee Theres than be president of anything. So I've got to figure out some way to make sure I lose."

The next day, Sunday, Ducky took a deep breath before she walked into church with her family. She wasn't sure how the other Bee Theres would greet her. She knew they'd met together the evening before to plan Marybeth's introduction.

Had they decided to throw her out of the Bee Theres? Would they all look the other way when she came into the chapel?

Becca and Elena were standing in the foyer talking when Ducky arrived. They came running over as soon as they saw her.

"Ducky," Elena said, "I've been dying to know what you're planning for your intro act tomorrow."

"We were trying to decide last night," Becca said, "whether you would ride out on an elephant like you did in that clothing commercial you did a while ago, or whether you'd get the school band to escort you out, or what?"

Ducky was so relieved that they were still friendly that she blurted out the truth before she even thought about it. "I don't know what my intro will be," she said. "Jamahl and Dermott and Anton are doing it. It's going to be a surprise to me."

The two girls looked puzzled. "You don't even know what it will be?" Becca said.

"Wow," Elena said. "You must trust your brothers a lot more than I trust mine."

"Well, it doesn't really . . ." Ducky stopped. She'd been going to say, "It doesn't really matter what they do." But she caught herself in time. She would have to be very careful not to make slips like that, not even give the girls a hint that she was planning to lose the election. Marybeth would be very hurt if she knew Ducky was trying to deliberately throw it.

"Doesn't really what?" Becca's eyes were slightly narrowed as she looked at Ducky. Did she guess what was going on?

"It doesn't really matter what I do for an intro,"

Ducky said. "Everybody knows Marybeth and they'll vote for her."

Becca seemed satisfied with that. "We're doing the cutest intro act for Marybeth," she said. "I wish you could join us."

"I do too," Ducky said truthfully.

It was time for sacrament meeting to start, so the other girls didn't get a chance to tell Ducky right then what the act would be. They all went to sit with their own families, so there wasn't any chance to find out during the meeting, but Ducky saw the other two mouthing words to Marybeth and Carlie when they came in during the organ prelude.

Sunshine was late, as usual. But as soon as she sat down, the other girls started sending signals to her, too.

Ducky felt left out.

When they all got to their Young Women's class, Becca told Sister Jackson right away about how both Marybeth and Ducky were running for seventh-grade class president.

Sister Jackson hesitated for only a moment before she said, "Well, isn't that nice. You'll all be fine examples, I'm sure." But her eyebrows were pulled together in a worried look.

Sister Jackson was pretty cool. She'd lived a long

time and knew a lot. If she was worried about how this was going to go, then Ducky was too.

But Sister Jackson's face smoothed out, and she said, "No matter which one of you wins, the seventh grade will have an excellent president. Congratulations to both of you." She cleared her throat. "Now, let's get on with our class. Marybeth, will you take over the opening exercises, please?"

Ducky relaxed as Marybeth asked Elena to give the opening prayer. She thought about how much fun it would have been to take part in Marybeth's intro act with the others. That made her wonder again what Jamahl, Anton, and Dermott were planning for her introduction.

What if they totally embarrassed her? Would she have to transfer to another junior high?

Ducky didn't even hear what Elena said in her opening prayer, and she was surprised when Marybeth said, "Ducky, you're next."

"Next?" Ducky didn't know what she was talking about.

Marybeth nodded. "With the scriptural passage."

Ducky had totally forgotten that she'd been asked to do the scriptural passage for the day. She didn't have anything prepared.

"Oh," she said, fumbling with her Bible. "Just a minute. I'll find it."

Nervously, she let the book fall open. Running her finger down the page, she landed on a familiar verse.

"First Corinthians, chapter 13," she said after a glance at the top of the page, "verse 12. 'For now we see through a glass, darkly; but then face to face: now I know in part; but then shall I know even as also I am known.'"

Uh-oh. Ducky swallowed. She thought of her Aunt Aleesha, who often opened the Bible and let her finger drop onto a random verse, hoping that it would somehow give her advice about whatever problem she was having.

That verse sounded almost like a warning.

# CHAPTER
8

The first thing Ducky saw when she got to school on Monday morning was Chester Burkey standing at the curb, handing out bright orange flyers to the kids as they arrived.

"Hi," he said shyly when she got close enough to hear. "Want one?" He held out a flyer, which was almost the same color as his hair and freckles.

Ducky took it. Uneven letters, hand printed across the top, spelled out the words "Don't be a turkey, vote for Burkey." Beneath the words was a photocopied snapshot of Chester that was almost too dark and fuzzy to recognize.

Ducky felt a little sorry for Chester. The flyer wasn't exactly an impressive beginning for his campaign.

She wished that Paula had chosen to manage

Chester's campaign instead of hers. Then Ducky wouldn't be in the crazy position of trying to lose the election, and Chester would have a better chance to win, with Powerhouse Paula planning things.

What was she thinking? She wanted *Marybeth* to win, not Chester.

"Thanks, Chester," she said. "It's a nice flyer."

Well, it was. In a way. The color was nice.

"Your posters are really funny," Chester said, blushing all the way to his hairline. "All the kids are going to love them."

"Thanks," Ducky said again.

She could see one of the posters that she and Jamahl had redecorated on Saturday. It wasn't supposed to be lovable. That wasn't the idea at all. The kids were supposed to think Ducky was too weird to vote for, what with the duck beak and all.

She was still looking at the poster when Paula descended on her like a tornado.

Paula held one of the posters up with both hands. "Ducky," she thundered, "did you see what somebody did to my posters? Somebody *ruined* them. Look at this."

*Her* posters.

Ducky took a deep breath. She knew she should have called Paula yesterday to tell her what she and Jamahl had done. She'd written in her diary last night that she was just too chicken to try to explain it over the phone. But taming Paula now would be like trying to undo a whirlwind.

"Uh, Paula," she began.

"I've told Mr. Dumont about it," Paula stormed. "He's coming out to look at the damage. Heads are going to roll."

Oh no. Ducky hadn't planned for her dad to get pulled into this.

"Paula," she said, making her voice strong this time. "I drew the duck beaks on the posters myself. Look, I signed each one so people would know I did it." She pointed to where she'd scribbled her name on the poster with Jamahl's marker.

Paula turned the poster so she could peer at it. Tracing the signature with a forefinger, she said, "You did this?"

From her tone, you would have thought that Ducky had done something really criminal, like torching the school or something.

"Yes." Ducky felt her vocal cords close off so that the word came out a mere squeak. Paula could be scary.

"*You* did this?" Paula repeated.

Ducky tried a shrug, but it came off more like a stiff twitch of her shoulder.

"I thought it would be funny," she squeaked.

"Y'know—my name and everything. Ducky. Duck beak. Y'know."

She was beginning to sound like Marybeth, who always fell into "y'knows" when she was nervous.

"Funny?" Paula's voice went up the scale.

Just then a group of kids passed by. "Great poster, Ducky," one of them yelled. The others grinned and waved friendly hands at her.

Paula stared after them.

Before she could say anything, Ducky's dad arrived.

"Okay, what's going on?" he asked. "What's this about posters being defaced?"

"Mr. Du*mont*." Paula turned to look at him. "For*give* me." She smiled sweetly into his face.

She had smoothly shifted gears. Ducky felt a little dizzy. She wasn't cut out for a life in politics, she decided. She'd better stick to ads and TV commercials—which seemed like a picnic compared to this.

Paula was still talking. "If I'd only *known* that Ducky had defaced her posters her*self*, I *never* would have bothered you." She shook her head slowly and lowered her eyes.

"Humph," Ducky's dad said.

Ducky knew that if *she'd* said what Paula had just said, her dad would have come back with something like, "It's pretty early in the season for a snow job like that."

But she didn't think he would say that to Paula.

"Humph," he said again. He took the poster, looking first at it and then at Ducky. "When did you do this, Miss Dumont?"

"Saturday, sir," she said. He was the Voice of Authority, the Principal. At times like this she felt as if she should address him as "sir."

He nodded. "Did you think through your reasons for doing it?"

"Yes, sir. I believe so, sir." Ducky's mouth felt dry.

He gazed for just a moment longer at Ducky, a little doubtfully, she thought. Then his gaze shifted to Paula. "And it goes down all right with you?"

"Oh yes, sir." Paula smiled again. "I didn't see the whole picture before, Mr. Dumont, sir. I mean, I didn't know . . ."

"You didn't know Ducky had done this herself," Ducky's dad finished for her. As he handed the poster back to Paula, he gave Ducky a look that said he was going to deliver the "Don't Be Impulsive" lecture to her again when they got home.

"I expect all of you to keep this election on a high plane," he said as he turned to leave. "No funny business."

"Yes, *sir*," Paula said. She looked as if she was

about to snap to attention and salute him. She watched him go. "I forgot he was your dad," she whispered.

Then, with a toss of her head, she changed back into the familiar Paula. "Well, I must say," she announced, "I underestimated you, Ducky. I hope your idea for your introduction works out as well as this did."

Ducky didn't say anything. The duck bill idea hadn't turned the kids off the way she'd planned. It had turned them *on*.

"Well?" Paula said. "You do have some kind of intro act prepared, don't you? Because if you don't my friends and I can still do our Power Ranger thing."

"I've got an act," Ducky said quickly.

"It better be good." Tucking the poster under her arm, Paula marched away.

Ducky felt a little limp. She hoped her intro act wouldn't be good.

But why was she worrying? Anton and Dermott would never miss an opportunity like this to trash her. And with Jamahl to see that it didn't go *too* far, she had nothing to worry about.

The seventh-grade campaign assembly was second period. All candidates for all offices and the people who were in their intro acts were supposed to assemble backstage in the auditorium right after first period.

Ducky saw the Bee Theres as soon as she got there. They were all dressed in frilly, old-fashioned pink dresses. They looked sweet and wholesome, which worried Ducky a little bit. If she'd been helping with Marybeth's campaign, she would have advised them to come up with something strictly nineties.

But Sunshine, Elena, Carlie, and Becca, as well as Marybeth, had lived in this area all their lives. Maybe they knew better what would go over well.

"Hi, Ducky," Marybeth said when she saw her. She was dressed in jeans and a shirt. She held onto a bicycle, which Ducky decided must be part of her act.

"I'm really looking forward to your intro act," Marybeth said. She looked around. "Who's doing it?"

Good question. Ducky didn't see Jamahl, Anton, or Dermott anywhere. Had they decided to back out on helping her lose the election? Maybe their big idea was simply not to show up, leaving her to flounder on her own. Maybe that was the best idea, after all.

"They'll be here," she told Marybeth. She looked at the other Bee Theres. "You look cute," she told them.

"We *are* cute," Becca said, and they all laughed.

Ducky laughed with them. "That's what I like. Modesty."

"It helps to keep up the confidence quotient." Marybeth held up a hand to show that it was shaking.

The other candidates were there backstage too. Chester Burkey was surrounded by a group of guys who were dressed as nerds. Or maybe they *were* nerds and were just looking normal. Ducky didn't know any of them except Chester.

Chester looked as if he'd rather be anywhere but there. It made Ducky wonder why he was running for seventh-grade class president. Had he been talked into it by somebody else, the way she had? Or did he really believe in what he was running for?

The other presidential candidate, Eddie Howland, had enough confidence for everybody. He wore a big smile and a hat that looked like the kind Shakey's Pizza Parlor gave out, with a red, white, and blue band around it. Surrounding him were several girls dressed in red, white, and blue costumes and tap shoes.

The introductions started with candidates for class treasurer and secretary. It took a while to get to the presidential candidates.

Eddie was the first one of them to be introduced.

A tuba quartet, all wearing hats like Eddie's, walked to the front of the stage and started playing

"Yankee Doodle Dandy." The girls in the red, white, and blue costumes tapped their way on stage.

The music had a fast march beat, and the girls really knew how to tap dance. The audience began clapping before they even finished their act. And when Eddie swung out to the middle of the stage on a rope, everybody cheered.

It was a fantastic intro. Ducky began to worry that Marybeth didn't have a chance against somebody like that.

"Those girls did that act at an all-city sixth-grade assembly last spring," Carlie whispered to Ducky. "They won some kind of award for it. Eddie recruited them from Evans Junior High to do his intro for him."

Eddie sounded like a real operator.

Next was Marybeth's act.

Elena's mother was at the piano in front of the stage. As she began playing, Becca, Carlie, Elena, and Sunshine strolled out, unfurling ruffled parasols and twirling them over their shoulders.

They started singing something about wouldn't anybody like to meet a sweet old-fashioned girl.

They looked pretty, but the song was so low-key after Eddie's act that Ducky was almost embarrassed for them.

But suddenly the tempo became really jazzy, and

the girls tossed away the parasols and began to do some peppy swing steps.

Out of the corner of her eye, Ducky saw Marybeth whip off the jeans and shirt she'd been wearing to reveal a bright green and black spandex biking suit with a cute little skirt. Clapping a black and green helmet on her head, she rode the bicycle onstage, circling through the other girls, who unfurled a banner that said, "Marybeth, a president for our times."

The kids in the audience yelled their approval.

Ducky was relieved. She didn't have to worry about Marybeth. She was going to handle this campaign just fine.

The Bee Theres came offstage breathless and laughing.

"You were *terrific*," Ducky said, hugging each one.

They scarcely saw Chester's act, which was something about computers. It got applause, but not anything wild and enthusiastic like the first two intros.

Then it was Ducky's turn. She didn't know where Jamahl, Anton, and Dermott had come from, but they suddenly appeared at her side, along with Augie Krump, Gregory Okinaga, and Arvy Dixon.

They were all dressed in yellow, feathery costumes from the Buck-a-Cluck Chicken Shack where Jamahl and Arvy worked. But instead of chicken heads, they wore wide, flat, orange duck beaks. On their feet were swimming flippers.

They looked completely, totally, one-hundred-percent ridiculous.

"Come out when we say 'Here she is, our next president,'" Jamahl whispered just before clumping onstage.

"Like when they announce Miss America," Dermott whispered, following Jamahl.

Ducky stared as the other guys went onstage too, their flipper fins flapping, their duck beaks snapping, their feathers quivering.

Someone started thumping on a piano, and since there wasn't anybody at the piano in front of the stage, Ducky guessed that the music was on tape. The guys must have made it on Saturday at Jamahl's house.

The music was "Old MacDonald had a farm," and the guys began doing a clumsy, clumpy dance as they sang, "Woodward Junior is so lucky, e-i-e-i-o; it's lucky 'cause it has a Ducky, e-i-e-i-o."

That was Dermott's cue to step forward and supply the quacks. "With a quack quack here, and a quack quack there . . ." The quacks were on the tape, too, making them twice as loud.

Nobody could quack like Dermott could. It was all so absolutely absurd that Ducky laughed aloud. This was a prime, number-one trash job. Nobody would vote for her after this.

Or so she thought before she heard the audience explode with laughter.

Then, before Ducky even went onstage, a chant started. "We want Ducky," it thundered. "We want Ducky, we want Ducky, we want Ducky."

# CHAPTER
# 9

After the assembly was over, kids came running up to tell Ducky that her intro act was the best ever. One kid called out, "Your act was a total success, Ducky."

But to Ducky it was a total failure.

It was supposed to have practically destroyed her chances of winning the election for seventh-grade class president.

Now, the way it looked, if the election were held that very day she would receive a lot of votes.

She tried to keep her smile turned up bright throughout all the congratulations, but she felt as if her batteries were wearing out.

It was especially difficult to keep smiling when Marybeth came over to hug her.

"I haven't laughed so hard in a long time,"

Marybeth said. "It's going to be so much fun having you for our president, Ducky."

"Hey, girl," Ducky said, holding Marybeth at arm's length and looking into her eyes. "Don't count my votes before they're hatched. I haven't won yet, not by a long way."

She examined Marybeth's face, trying to detect any hidden anger. She didn't see any indications that Marybeth hated her, although she wouldn't have blamed her if she did.

"Everybody's going to vote for you," Marybeth predicted.

"You think they're going to forget that great act of yours?" Ducky asked. "You know what I was wishing while I watched the other Bee Theres perform? I wished I was out there with them, boppin' around that stage. I wanted to be a part of it too."

Marybeth nodded. "That would have been great, Ducky. I wish you could have been with them."

That was as close as Marybeth came to any regrets about the assembly. She seemed genuinely happy that Ducky had made such a good impression.

That made things a little easier.

Anton and Dermott came to say they had to rush off to their own schools.

They said something more, but there was so much noise out on the stage that Ducky couldn't hear it. So she just returned the high fives they gave her and smiled a good-bye as they left.

The noise was mostly Eddie Howland's tuba quartet oompah-oompahing and a group of his supporters yelling to Eddie how great he was. Eddie was yelling back, too, mostly jokes. As Ducky listened, he yelled, "Knock, knock."

"Who's there?" hollered a bunch of kids.

"Farley."

"Farley who?"

Eddie threw his arms into the air. "Farley me, I'm your leader."

There was a lot of laughing and arm punching.

"You're the greatest, Eddie," somebody bellowed.

"I know, I know," Eddie admitted and did a triumphant little jig around the stage.

Ducky almost wished she really was running for president. It would be such a pleasure to try to beat somebody like Eddie.

He was conceited, but in an effort to be friendly Ducky waved, making a circle with her thumb and forefinger to indicate that his act was great.

She was sure Eddie saw her, but he didn't wave back.

Not too many people were congratulating Chester Burkey. He and his friends stood off to one side, talking quietly to one another.

Ducky wasn't sure quite what she would say, but she made her way to him, accepting more congratulations as she went.

"Hey, Chester," she said, patting him on the back. "What a neat idea, building your act around computers. Really up-to-date, nineties stuff."

Chester seemed genuinely impressed that Ducky came over to talk to him.

"Thanks." A bashful grin rearranged his freckles. "That's what my whole campaign is going to be about. I'm going to push for more computers and other equipment for our school. That'll be my platform."

Ducky hadn't thought much about what her platform would be. Maybe she should just let Paula take care of that. Ducky hadn't been too successful in trashing herself. Maybe Paula could do a better job.

Where *was* Paula, anyway? Not that Ducky wanted to see her, but it was odd that she wasn't right there soaking up the congratulations, even though the act hadn't been her idea.

Ducky became aware that Chester was still talking. He was telling her how funny her intro act had been. "I wish I could think of something like that," he said. "I need to lighten up, or nobody will vote for me."

Ducky forced a laugh. "And *I* need to *un*lighten a little, or nobody will take me seriously."

She was going to say something encouraging to Chester, but Paula arrived just then. She pounced on Ducky, announcing in a loud voice that she'd been hanging around the halls, listening to reactions.

"All I heard was 'Ducky, Ducky, Ducky,'" she said. "There really wasn't any competition."

Ducky wished Paula hadn't said that in front of Chester.

Paula didn't even appear to see Chester. He seemed to be beneath her notice.

"Paula," Ducky said, "I thought everybody did well today."

Paula shrugged. "Oh well, Eddie was okay. But we'll slime him somehow before election day. We'll be running this place before anybody knows what happened to them," she finished.

There it was again. The "we" stuff. Ducky was the one running for president, but it was looking as if Paula planned to run Ducky.

"By the way," Paula said, "I want you to take this." She held up a small notebook. "Be careful with it. It's a list of strategies I plan to use to win this election. I want you to go over them and give me some input, since you seem to have a feel for this kind of thing."

"I do?" said Ducky.

Paula nodded. "I wouldn't have given two cents for your intro act when you said you were going to plan it. But it was right on target with what the kids like. Ducky, you're off and running."

Shoving the little notebook into Ducky's limp hand, she said, "I'll call you later," and marched away.

Ducky put the notebook in her book bag as she watched Paula parade up the corridor. She really ought to be running, all right. Running away from Paula. Running away from running for president.

Run, Ducky, run.

It wasn't until the end of the next period that Ducky remembered she hadn't seen Jamahl after the intro acts. She watched for him all day, but he seemed to have disappeared.

Why hadn't he come up to say something to her?

She didn't see Marybeth and the other Bee Theres, either, until the end of the school day when they walked out of the building just ahead of her. They were talking and laughing together, and Ducky felt left out again.

Shifting her book bag from one shoulder to the other, she felt sorry once more that she had agreed when Paula first asked her to run for class president.

But there was no way to make that unhappen, nor to change any of the other things that had taken place since she'd made the decision to run. It didn't do any good to go over and over things that had already happened.

The thing to figure out now was what to do from now on, in order to lose the election.

Maybe she could get some ideas from Paula's list of strategies. Maybe she could make some of them backfire.

She was reaching back into her book bag to get Paula's little notebook when Carlie turned around.

"There you are, Ducky," she called. "We've been looking for you. Come on, catch up with us."

The other Bee Theres stopped, and Carlie reached out a welcoming hand as Ducky hurried to catch up to the circle of Bee Theres.

They all greeted her warmly.

"I guess we've got our work cut out for us," Elena said, "trying to pump ourselves up to compete with that team of yours." She laughed when she said it, but Ducky wondered if there wasn't just a hint of criticism.

No, Elena wasn't one to make subtle jabs like that. If she was upset, she would come right out and say it.

"Listen," Ducky said, "I wouldn't trust that team of mine as far as I can toss them. There's no telling what they might do to me."

There. That might prepare them for the trash job Ducky hoped for as the campaign rolled along. They would think it was her team's fault and wouldn't suspect that she was deliberately trying to lose.

Becca rolled her eyes. "No telling what *we* might do to *Marybeth,* either. We're a little worried, now that we've seen the competition."

Ducky linked arms with her as they all started walking again.

"Well, don't think of me as competition," she said. "I'm just one of the Bee Theres."

Marybeth, who was walking ahead, spoke over her shoulder. "We were heading to McDonald's for a little snack. Want to join us? We're going to plan my platform."

Ducky didn't know what to say. "Do you think I should?" she asked. "I mean, *me* being in on the planning of *your* platform?"

"We don't think of you as competition. Just one of the Bee Theres." Sunshine was mimicking Ducky's own words.

Ducky laughed. "Right. I'd love to join you."

The main plank in Marybeth's platform, Ducky discovered as they munched on burgers and fries, was the celebration of different ethnic holidays.

"How many nationalities do we have represented at Woodward Junior High?" Marybeth asked. "We need to find out. Then we can do some research on what holidays are important to each group."

"I can supply you with all the info you need on

Kwanzaa," Ducky said. "That's an African-American holiday."

"Great." Elena sounded enthusiastic. "Maybe we could have a day where everybody wears the clothes of their original country, like the Bee Theres did at our ancestors party."

That had been the first Beehive class party Ducky attended after she moved to Pasadena. Even within their own little group of six, there had been six nationalities represented.

"That's such a good thing to do," she told Marybeth. "The kids will have a lot of fun and everybody will benefit from remembering their roots."

She realized she sounded like Sister Jackson.

But what was wrong with that? It was true.

She wished she had thought of a platform like Marybeth's.

No, something like that would really appeal to the kids. It would bring a lot of votes. She didn't *want* a lot of votes.

She kept forgetting that.

She wanted to *lose* the election.

"What's your platform going to be?" Marybeth asked, breaking into Ducky's thoughts.

"I don't know," Ducky confessed. "This is all new to me, you guys. Remember, I hadn't even planned to run until last Friday when Paula asked me to. I haven't thought a lot about platforms. Paula's going to help me with it."

The Bee Theres all looked at her.

"Do you need Paula?" Becca asked. "A lot of kids are turned off by her. Why don't you just stick with Jamahl and your brother and those other guys?"

That was the second time they'd hinted that they didn't think much of Paula.

But if Paula turned kids off, that was to Ducky's advantage, wasn't it? She'd better stick with her. She wanted to *lose* the election.

"Paula's my campaign manager," Ducky said. "I guess she's thinking about what my campaign platform will be."

"She'd better think fast," Becca said. "You have to give a three-minute speech at tomorrow's assembly."

Ducky sighed. "Don't I know it."

"Look." Marybeth leaned forward. "If you have any problems with Paula—or with planning your platform—call us. In fact, I'll try to call you later tonight. We're the Bee Theres. We'll be there for you."

Ducky felt relieved. She knew the other Bee Theres would help her if she needed it. "You guys are terrific," she said.

Ducky felt good as the Bee Theres parted after their meeting at McDonald's. Although they'd all agreed when she'd first confessed she was running that it would make no difference to their friendship, she had wondered occasionally if it might.

Certainly there had been no strain at the meeting. They had offered to help her, and she'd said she would contribute something to Marybeth's holiday platform.

After she said good-bye to the other Bee Theres, Ducky headed for home. As she passed by Sister Truesdale's street, she decided to drop in. Sister Truesdale had invited her to come by anytime, and right now she needed to talk over a few things with somebody who wasn't all that much involved in her life.

Billy Goat Gruff met her at the gate, just as he had the other time she'd been there. Fixing his odd eyes on her, he bleated a greeting, and as soon as she opened the gate, he began nibbling at her again, delicately tasting the hem of her shirt, then shifting to the book bag.

Ducky let him chew. The book bag was heavy denim. She didn't think he could hurt it.

She expected Sister Truesdale to answer the door, but instead it was Jamahl.

His face drooped when he saw her.

"Ducky," he said. "I'm really sorry about that intro act."

Sister Truesdale came up behind him.

"Come in, Ducky," she said. "Jamahl was just telling me about it all, about how you all tried to fail but were a great success instead." She motioned for Ducky to sit in one of the wing chairs by the fireplace.

Gruff followed her there, and when she set down her book bag he resumed his chewing. She shooed him away and he retreated, but he kept his eyes on the bag.

Ducky turned to Jamahl. "Is that why I didn't see you all day?" she asked. "I mean, because you thought I'd be mad about the intro being a success?"

He nodded. "I'm sorry."

"Don't be sorry," she said. "We still have time to make me lose. You guys should feel good about how much everybody liked what you did."

He nodded glumly.

"Besides," she said, "maybe neither Marybeth nor I have anything to worry about. Maybe Eddie will sweep the elections. *He* thinks he will."

Sister Truesdale nodded. "Jamahl told me about him, too. Eddie seems kind of stuck on himself. Back in Wyoming we used to say that some roosters think the sun comes up just to hear them crow."

Ducky laughed, and even Jamahl smiled.

"The next thing coming up is the speech tomorrow where I have to say what my platform is. Maybe you should help me with that, too." She looked at

Jamahl. "Do you have any ideas that would be kind of far out? I want to think of something that will turn the kids off."

Jamahl looked thoughtful, then shook his head. "Better let Paula help you on that one. She'll have lots of ideas."

"Well," Ducky said. "Paula does have some ideas. She gave me her notebook of strategies. I'll see if there's something I can use."

She reached for her book bag to pull out Paula's little notebook. It wasn't by the side of the chair.

Neither was Gruff.

"Oh, no," Ducky groaned.

It wasn't hard to imagine what had happened.

# CHAPTER
# 10

Ducky, Jamahl, and Sister Truesdale found Gruff in the kitchen. The book bag lay on the floor. There was a corner chewed out of its top, and its contents were strewn around the floor.

The little notebook Paula had given to Ducky was gone, except for a scrap of the front cover. The scrap had part of Paula's name on it: "Paula Pow," it said.

"Pow is right," Ducky groaned. "How am I going to tell Paula a goat ate her campaign strategy notebook? She told me to guard it with my life. What am I going to say?"

Jamahl and Sister Truesdale gazed silently at the scene before them. The only sound was Gruff's munching and swallowing. Probably the last page of the notebook was right now sliding down his throat.

Finally Sister Truesdale spoke. "Why not the truth?"

Jamahl folded his hands into his armpits, making his arms like wings. "Pock-pock-pock-pock-pock," he said.

"I'm too chicken," Ducky admitted.

"Paula's a real pistol," Jamahl said in explanation.

There was another stretch of silence, then Sister Truesdale cleared her throat. "Back home in Wyoming folks used to say, 'If you have a choice, be smart. If you don't have a choice, be brave.' Seems to me there's nowhere to go but straight at it."

"I didn't even read the notebook," Ducky mourned. "I don't even know which of Paula's ideas were good."

"Or bad," Jamahl said. He stared gloomily at the goat. "We oughta make Gruff tell Paula himself."

"Sure," Ducky said, picturing herself dragging the goat to school to confront Paula.

Suddenly she clapped her hands. "Jamahl, you're a genius! That's *exactly* what we're going to do."

Jamahl's eyes widened. "*What's* what we're going to do?"

"I'm going to let Gruff tell Paula what he did," Ducky said. "That is, if Sister Truesdale will loan him to us for a day."

"You can't take him on campus," Jamahl said. "Remember, there are rules against animals."

Ducky was grateful to him for mentioning that. She didn't want to get in hot water with her dad for breaking the school rules.

"I'll just take him to the edge of the campus," she said. "I just want to show Paula where her notebook went. She can't get too mad at a sweet guy like him."

Sister Truesdale was looking interested. "Gruff would love to go," she said. "When is it you want him?"

"Second period tomorrow," Ducky said. "The seventh grade will be having an assembly out on the lawn where the candidates will give three-minute speeches about what their platforms will be."

"I'll have him there," Sister Truesdale said. With a grin she added, "And I think maybe I'll stay for the assembly."

"Thanks a lot, Sister Truesdale," Ducky said, gathering up the rest of her things and stuffing them into the mangled book bag. "I'll see you tomorrow, then." Gruff burped softly as she gave him a farewell pat.

To Ducky's surprise, Jamahl offered to walk home with her. She accepted happily.

"What are you going to talk about in your three minutes?" Jamahl asked as they walked along.

"I don't know," Ducky said. "I was hoping to get some ideas from Paula's little book."

Jamahl didn't question her any further. He kicked a rock off the sidewalk as they walked along. "Ducky, you could easy win this election, if you wanted to. I wish we didn't have to make you lose. You'd be a primo president."

He looked at her shyly as he spoke.

"Next year," Ducky said. "Maybe I'll run again then, for real. But this year is Marybeth's. That's the way I want it," she added when Jamahl looked as if he might protest.

But she couldn't help feeling how great it would be just to ride into office on the wave of popularity that Jamahl and Anton and Dermott had created for her that day.

At dinner that night, Anton and Dermott were also apologetic about their act, but not very much.

"We were great," Dermott told Ducky's mom. He turned to exchange a high five with Anton.

"We're so great we can't fail even when we try," Anton agreed, and the two of them exchanged another high five.

"They really were funny, Mom," Ducky said. She hated to give them credit when she knew it would inflate their heads even bigger than they already were. But it was the truth.

Mom grinned, but there was a little worry line between her eyes. "What did your father think about it?" she asked.

Dad was working late at the junior high that night. He hadn't yet come home.

"Oh," Dermott said, "Uncle Walter laughed as much as anybody else. I was watching him."

Ducky had noticed before that Dermott frequently watched her dad to see what his reactions would be. It was as if Dermott thought he might be kicked out of their house if his uncle became displeased about things he did.

It must be hard living with a family that was not really your own, especially when you had no idea when you might get together again with your own mom. Ducky felt a little sorry for Dermott, even though he was being his usual obnoxious self at the moment, loudly showing Mom how he'd quacked at the assembly.

"When can we do it again?" he asked Ducky when he'd finished his demonstration. "It was really fun. I've got the tape we made right here, if you need it."

"I don't need it tomorrow," Ducky told him. "Tomorrow's when I give a speech about what I'll do if I get elected."

Dermott looked disappointed.

"But I'll tell you what I'll do. I'll take the tape with me, just in case," Ducky told him. "Put it in my book bag."

He looked happier. "What *will* you do if you get elected?" he asked.

Ducky was tired of thinking about it. "I'm going to let my campaign manager decide."

"You mean Paula?" Anton asked.

Ducky nodded.

This time Anton put up a hand to exchange a high five with *her*. "You should have let her take over in the first place, if trashing is what you want," he said.

"You know Paula?"

"I know her brother Dave. I've been at their house. She's got a tongue like a chain saw."

That was a little intimidating to hear. But maybe things were going to work out.

Paula called right after dinner.

"Tell me what you've decided," she demanded as soon as Ducky said "Hello." "Which of my ideas are you going to use for your platform?"

Ducky hadn't expected Paula to call until later in the evening, after Ducky had had a chance to figure out just exactly what she would say to her. Ducky

95

hadn't even thought through how she would tell about the destroyed notebook.

Certainly she couldn't do it over the phone.

She felt her heart speed up. Even from several miles away, Paula was scary.

Ducky took a deep breath. "What I've decided is to let you explain my platform, Paula," she said. "I'll say a few words, then turn it over to you."

Maybe that was all she needed to say right now.

"It's about time," Paula said. "I'm glad you've finally realized what I can do for you."

"Me too," Ducky said. "I know that whatever you do will be what I need, Paula."

That was the truth. If what she'd been hearing was true, *anything* Paula did would make the kids cross Ducky off their candidate list.

"Well." Paula sounded pleased. "Maybe I'd better come get my campaign strategies notebook so I can make plans."

"Oh no," Ducky said, realizing that she sounded nervous—which she was, but she didn't want Paula asking questions. "I mean, I might not be here."

She might go to a movie.

She might go for a walk.

She might call an emergency meeting of the Bee Theres.

She might blast off to Mars.

Anything to not be around if Paula was coming over.

What if Paula asked her to read something from the notebook? Ducky held her breath.

But all Paula said was, "You'll have it with you tomorrow. That's soon enough. I remember most of what was in it anyway."

"Yes." Ducky nodded even though she knew Paula couldn't see her over the phone. "Yes, I'll have it with me."

She didn't tell Paula it would be inside Gruff.

The phone rang again as soon as Paula hung up. Ducky thought it would be Marybeth calling, as she'd said she would do. But instead it was Stormi LaBelle, who booked jobs in ads and commercials for her.

"Can you do a shoot on Saturday?" Stormi asked. "It'll be right there at your own school in Pasadena, so it's not like a travel. You won't miss any school days."

Too bad, Ducky thought. She wouldn't mind being away for a while right now.

"Yes," she said. "What'll I need?"

"Mainly your feet," Stormi said. "It's for a sports shoe. As I understand it, you'll be wearing an African robe and the voice-over will talk about how people everywhere love this particular sports shoe. The details aren't worked out yet. You know what a last-minute guy Syd is. I'll let you know."

Syd was the director Ducky had worked with on several previous commercials. He really was a last-minute guy, but he called it spontaneity.

Ducky said she could do the commercial and was about to hang up when Stormi said, "Syd mentioned that he thinks he'd like to use a bunch of average kids in the background. Do you think some of your friends could qualify?"

"Yes," she said quickly. "Tell him I can get as many kids as he wants." The Bee Theres would love it!

"Great. He'll probably be calling you."

After Stormi hung up, Ducky thought about calling the Bee Theres immediately to ask it they'd like to be in the shoe commercial.

But wouldn't that seem like she was trying to bribe her way back into their friendship?

Marybeth had said she would call later to find out if Ducky needed the Bee Theres to help her draw up her platform.

She decided to wait until then to say anything.

Marybeth didn't call.


The next day Ducky found Sister Truesdale and Gruff waiting at the curb on the edge of the school property.

Ducky wasn't so sure anymore that having Gruff come was a good idea. What if Paula turned her chain-saw tongue on him?

Ducky patted Gruff on the head and he was nibbling at the pocket of her jeans when Paula came along.

"There you are, Ducky," she said. "I need my notebook." Her eyes flicked without interest over Sister Truesdale, then rested on Gruff. "What's this reeking beast doing here?"

"He brought your notebook," Ducky said.

Paula looked blank.

"He ate it," Ducky explained.

"He *what*?" Paula flashed from calm to tornado warning.

"Ate it," Ducky said. "He ate your notebook."

Paula looked at Gruff as if her eyes could tear him apart and retrieve her property. "This is the *stupidest* thing I ever *heard*," she screeched. "I *demand* that you get my notebook from him."

Ducky pretended to look perplexed. "Well, I guess I could stick my finger down his throat, but I don't think you'd be able to read much of what comes up."

Paula began to sputter like a firecracker, and Ducky was afraid there was going to be a major explosion.

But Paula apparently noticed that a lot of kids

were coming over to admire Gruff, because she totally shifted gears. She looked at the kids, then looked at Gruff. You could almost hear the wheels turning in her head.

"It was nice of you to bring him, Ducky," she purred. "Is he going to stay around for a while?"

For the first time Sister Truesdale spoke. "I thought he'd enjoy watching the proceedings."

Paula gave a tinkly little laugh. "He'll enjoy seeing Ducky triumph again. Did you hear about how well things went yesterday?"

"Ducky told me," Sister Truesdale said.

"It'll be even better today." Paula patted Gruff gingerly on the head. "I have to run along and figure out what I'm going to say, now that this lovely fellow swallowed my notebook." With a glance at Ducky, she hurried away.

The seventh-grade presidential candidates had drawn straws earlier to determine the order in which they would appear. Ducky was last again.

Chester was first. He delivered a real yawner of a speech about how much the school needed new computers and other equipment to prepare the students for the world they would be facing in a few years.

Marybeth's speech was terrific. There was a lot of clapping as she mentioned the various cultures in their school and how much they could learn from one another if they celebrated the holidays of the many countries.

Eddie had his tuba quartet there again, this time punctuating the points of his speech with blats of march music. Ducky wasn't exactly sure what his platform was when he finished, but he *had* been exciting to listen to.

Then it was Ducky's turn. Smiling at Sister Truesdale and Gruff, who still stood at the edge of the school property, she walked out onto the stage.

She paused for just a moment to get everybody's attention. Then she pointed at Gruff and said, "You've all heard about the Three Billy Goats Gruff. Well, that billy goat over there is gruff this morning because he ate my platform."

"Ba-a-a-a-a-ah," Gruff bleated from the sidelines.

The audience hooted with laughter and kids stood up to get a better look at the goat.

"Therefore," Ducky said, "I'm going to let Paula, my campaign manager, tell you all about what we have in mind."

She expected Paula to leap up on stage and take over. But she was walking across the lawn toward Sister Truesdale and Gruff.

As the whole seventh grade watched, Paula took Gruff's leash from a surprised Sister Truesdale and

started yanking him across the grass toward the platform.

Ducky was surprised too. She hadn't planned on
this. Numbly she stood and watched Paula and Gruff
approach.

# CHAPTER
# 11

Paula led the goat right up to the platform. He tried to hold back when they came to the three stairs, planting his feet in the grass and dragging backwards against the leash. His mouth opened and shut as if he were trying to bleat, but the leash must have been cutting off his breath because no sound came out.

He was no match for Paula. She kept jerking him until he had to come up the stairs.

Ducky wanted to yell for Paula to stop. What about the rule about animals on campus? Didn't Paula know about that?

But it was too late to stop it now. Gruff was already on campus. In fact, he was already on the platform.

He calmed down a little when Paula stopped pulling at him after settling him in front of the mike. Gazing out over the crowd of seventh graders, he opened his mouth. "Ba-a-a-a-ah," he said, as if expressing an opinion.

The kids loved it. They laughed, they hooted, they yelled their approval.

Ducky watched in dismay. Why hadn't she thought ahead and figured out that Paula might use Gruff? She should have known from the way Paula had been looking at him.

How was she going to explain to Dad about bringing a goat on campus? Technically, she'd brought him only to the *edge* of the campus, but Dad probably wouldn't see it that way. "Impulsive," he would say. "Ducky, how often have I warned you not to be impulsive?"

Any way you looked at it, she was in deep weeds.

She was obviously also headed toward being the favorite candidate, from the way the kids were reacting.

"Ducky," they screamed. "Ducky, Ducky, Ducky."

The noise finally died down enough for Paula to speak.

"Here," Paula hollered into the mike, "is the goat who ate the papers that contained the notes that explained the planks that made up the platform . . ."

"That lived in the house that Ducky built," somebody yelled, and everybody hooted and whistled again.

Ducky was aware that Sister Truesdale had come up to stand beside her.

"I'm right sorry," she said. "That girl snatched Gruff's leash away before I could get my wits about me. I didn't mean for it to happen."

Ducky nodded. "I know." She put an arm around Sister Truesdale, who was shaking her head mournfully.

"I should have given more thought to what might happen if I brought Gruff here," Sister Truesdale whispered. "Back in Wyoming we used to say, 'Before you go into a canyon, know how you'll get out.'"

Ducky knew her dad would like that one. She'd tell it to him sometime.

But not until this whole thing was far in the past.

Paula was still talking up there on the platform. "If we had Superman eyes," she yelled, "we'd see that those notes inside Gruff's big belly say that Ducky plans to bring more seventh-grade clout to the Student Council. We're the new kids on the block, but that doesn't mean we can't have a big say in student government if we demand it." She shot a fist into the air. "And Ducky is going to *demand* it."

"Ba-a-a-a-a-ah," said Gruff. He reached over to chew on the edge of Paula's shirt, but then stopped and shook his head as if she tasted bad.

The kids went crazy, and Paula waved her arm like

an orchestra conductor, encouraging them to yell even more.

Sister Truesdale looked questioningly at Ducky. "Demand?" she whispered. "That doesn't sound like you."

"This is all news to me," Ducky whispered back.

She knew what Paula really meant. *Paula* was going to be making the demands, using Ducky's mouth. Ducky pictured herself as a ventriloquist's dummy, sitting on Paula's knee, her mouth opening and closing as Paula said the words.

She didn't even hear what the other planks of her platform were, as they appeared to Paula's X-ray eyes through Gruff's thick hide. She didn't hear because she had caught sight of Marybeth and the girls from her Beehive class. They stood off to one side in a little clump, and they huddled together as if they were protecting themselves from an outside enemy. They were the Bee Theres, and they were there for Marybeth.

She, Ducky, was that outside enemy.

The nightmarish assembly finally finished.

Paula, flushed with victory, brought Gruff back to Sister Truesdale, who immediately left with him after telling Ducky to drop by her house after school.

"Ducky," Paula said, "it was absolutely brilliant of you to think up this thing about the goat eating your platform. Nothing I had planned would have gone over half as well."

She spoke as if Ducky had plotted the whole thing. Maybe she really thought Ducky had planned that things would work out the way they did.

But more likely she was just sliding away from the blame for bringing the goat onto campus, in case Ducky's dad should object.

It was hard to know with Paula.

"Now," Paula said, "for the rest of the week we just do as much campaigning as we can, then we vote on Monday. You're a sure winner right now, Ducky, and we don't want to take a chance on anything changing that. So I'll handle everything from now on."

In other words, she was telling Ducky to stay out of her own campaign. After all, it wasn't really Ducky who was running for president. It was Paula. Ducky knew that now.

She opened her mouth to object, but before she spoke she remembered what Anton had said the day before. He'd said she should have let Paula run her campaign in the first place, if she wanted to be trashed.

That hadn't seemed to be the case today. But it was the only hope left now.

"Okay, Paula," Ducky said. "It's all yours."

It was kind of a relief to just let it go and hope Paula would flub somehow.

"By the way," Paula said, "will you get that quacking tape from your brother? We may want to use it."

A tape from Anton? It took Ducky a moment to figure out what Paula was talking about.

"Oh," she said, "you mean the one Dermott made. He's my cousin, not my brother."

Paula shrugged. "Whatever." She clearly wasn't interested in Ducky's family relationships.

"It's in my book bag, which is in my locker. I'll give it to you after school, unless you need it now."

"After school's fine," Paula said as she hurried away.

Kids whacked Ducky on the back as they headed for classes. They told her how great it was to have her there at Woodward Junior High.

"The best thing that's happened since the chem lab blew up," one guy said as he passed.

Yeah, right. A disaster, that's what she was.

Ducky tried to grin as kids congratulated her, but she was looking for the other Bee Theres. They might have gone right to class.

She didn't find the Bee Theres, but she did see Jamahl. His face was glum.

"Paula's smarter than we are," he said.

Ducky didn't argue. "Did you see Marybeth and

Sunshine and the others?" she asked. "I can't find them."

"I saw them." Jamahl looked even glummer than before. "They didn't talk to me."

Ducky groaned, and Jamahl nodded.

"You don't have to stick with me," Ducky told him. "I don't want you to lose all your friends just because I'm an outcast."

Jamahl looked surprised. "I'll stand by you, Ducky," he said, "no matter what happens."

His face rearranged itself into a shy grin as he turned to hurry off to his class.

Ducky didn't see the Bee Theres again until after school. She was standing with Paula just outside the main door, digging in her book bag for the quacking tape, when all five girls came around the corner of the building. Marybeth, Sunshine, Becca, Elena, and Carlie. All together. Friends united in a cause.

Against her.

She tried on a smile. "Hi," she said.

"Hi," the others echoed.

They smiled too.

"Hi," Paula said.

She didn't smile.

Nobody said anything.

"Well," Marybeth said finally. "I guess we'd better go. We've got a lot to do."

Paula pocketed the tape. "Me too." She punched Ducky softly on the arm. "We've got it made," she said as she left. "No competition."

She said it softly, but still loud enough for everybody to hear.

The Bee Theres turned to go too.

Ducky was embarrassed at what Paula had said right in front of them. She longed to tell them to stop, wait, let her say what was really going on, that she was trying to throw the election, that she hoped Paula would snarl things up so the kids wouldn't vote for Ducky.

But if the truth would have hurt Marybeth before, it would devastate her now. It would say to her that Ducky thought the same way Paula did, that Marybeth had no chance of winning if Ducky stayed in the race.

Either way, Ducky would be left in cold outer darkness, away from the warmth and friendship of the Bee Theres.

She reached a hand out toward them. "You've got such good ideas," she said desperately, then realized how it sounded. It was the equivalent of a pat on the head.

The girls stopped.

"The goat was funny," Carlie said.

Kind little Carlie, who always found something

good to say in any situation. It must have been a strain in this one.

They stood there for a moment. Ducky had the impression that they were reaching out to her, but they didn't move.

"Well," Marybeth said a second time, "I guess we'd better go."

Ducky wished they'd invite her to go with them, to help plan Marybeth's next move the way they'd done before. They were probably going to McDonald's.

"I have to go too," Ducky said. "See you later."

"See you later" echoed around the circle of Bee Theres as they started down the street.

Together.

Ducky watched them go.

Alone.

# CHAPTER
# 12

Ducky headed for Sister Truesdale's house. When she got there, she found Gruff waiting at the gate as if he were expecting her.

"Ba-a-a-a-ah," he bleated as she opened the gate. "Ba-a-a-a-a-a-ah!" His little beard trembled indignantly.

Was he trying to tell her something? Was he saying Paula had used him, just as she was trying to use Ducky?

Ducky patted his head and scratched behind his ears. "It's okay, Gruff. It wasn't your fault."

She knew whose fault it was. It was hers. She was to blame for everything going wrong and for losing her best friends.

But she didn't want to think about it. It was like when she and Anton and Dermott played Monopoly.

No use feeling bad about landing on a square that cost you all your houses and hotels. It was time to move on, to pass "Go" again and see what you could do about your losses.

Sister Truesdale appeared at her open door as Ducky, with Gruff's teeth attached to the edge of her jeans pocket, walked up the stairs of the porch.

"I'm glad you could come, Ducky," Sister Truesdale said, holding the screen door open. "Seems like I helped to get you into this fix, so I should help pry you out."

She shooed at Gruff to stop him from eating Ducky's clothes. "Sit down," she said. "I'll get us some refreshments."

She shooed at Gruff again, then headed for the kitchen.

Gruff stopped chewing, but he stood by Ducky's chair, watching her through his golden eyes with the elongated, horizontal pupils.

Did those odd eyes see things the same way she did? Or was everything stretched, distorted, twisted because his eyes were different?

Were her own eyes different? Was she seeing things in a different way from how the other Bee Theres saw them? Were they rejecting her because she was chewing up Marybeth's chances of winning the election—or for some other reason?

Maybe they hadn't wanted her as a member of the Bee Theres in the first place and were taking this opportunity to dump her. After all, she'd come roaring into their lives like a runaway freight train and had been rolling full bore down the tracks ever since.

Maybe they wanted to go back to the way they were before she cycloned into town.

"No wonder they hate me," she said aloud. "I've been doing it all wrong from the beginning."

Sister Truesdale was coming back from the kitchen with a pitcher of fresh lemonade and glasses on a tray. "What was that you said?"

"I'm just one big mistake," Ducky said gloomily. "I've made one mistake after another ever since I set foot in this town."

Sister Truesdale set the tray down on a little table next to her chair. "Back in Wyoming we always said that another word for mistakes is experience. How else does a body get to know anything except by learning from our mistakes?" She poured out a glass of lemonade and handed it to Ducky. Pouring one for herself, she sat down. "Now, what are these tree-sized clubs you're bashing yourself with?"

Between sips of lemonade Ducky told Sister Truesdale about all her failings.

Sister Truesdale wouldn't have any of it. "Pshaw," she said. Ducky noticed that she pronounced it "Puhshaw." She'd seen the word in print but had never heard anybody say it. "Pshaw, Ducky, you got it all wrong. Those girls think the world and more of you. Why, Becca told me one day that you were the best thing that's come into their lives since Big Macs."

"She did?" Ducky was flattered. Becca loved those Big Macs. She stuffed them into her tiny frame as if she had a warehouse inside her.

"She did." Sister Truesdale nodded. "Those girls love you. It's time to finish up this little pity party and get on to thinking about what you're going to do next."

Gruff moved close enough to nibble on Ducky's bare arm. It was like a caress, as if he were saying he loved her too.

"What do you see as your next move?" Sister Truesdale went on. "What's coming up in the campaign?"

Ducky was beginning to feel better. "Just small stuff. The candidates hold little lawn rallies and hand out stuff to remind people to vote for them."

"And what are you going to hand out?" Sister Truesdale held up the lemonade pitcher to offer Ducky some more.

Ducky shrugged. "I don't know. Paula is going to handle that," she said.

Sister Truesdale nodded slowly. "How do you feel about that?"

"Well . . ." Ducky hesitated. "Remember what Jamahl said about Paula? He says she'll probably do something that will turn all the kids off so they won't vote for me."

"Is that what you want?" Sister Truesdale asked.

"I want them to vote for Marybeth." Ducky thought about it. "But if they vote for her because they hate Paula, that isn't really voting *for* her, is it?"

"Is it?" Sister Truesdale echoed.

"No." Ducky answered her own question. "It's voting against Paula. I mean, against me."

"What about the other candidates?" Sister Truesdale asked.

Ducky thought about Eddie and Chester. "Eddie's stirring up a lot of excitement. But it's hard to say whether that'll get the most votes for him."

"And the other boy?" Sister Truesdale prompted.

"Chester? He's got some really good ideas." What else could she say about him?

"So basically it comes down to being between you and Marybeth." Sister Truesdale seemed to be summing things up. "And you've been trying to help Marybeth win by making yourself out a loser."

"It hasn't worked," Ducky said.

She watched Gruff move another step closer, then

lower his head to chew on the laces of her Reeboks. It reminded her of the shoe commercial she was going to do on the campus on Saturday. That would probably attract a lot of attention and might make even more kids vote for her.

But she couldn't turn down a chance for work. They might not ask her the next time they had something.

Sister Truesdale was totally silent. She seemed to be waiting for Ducky to figure it out.

"I guess I should just let things go the way they're going to go," Ducky said. What was it that Mr. Sanchez was always saying in her Spanish class? "Qué será, será," she added. What will be, will be.

"Or?"

Or what? What was Sister Truesdale trying to get her to say? She could just let things drift, or she could . . . what?

"Or I could do something to help Marybeth," she said.

Sister Truesdale nodded.

Ducky remembered that right at the first she and Marybeth had said they would run a campaign where the candidates were friendly and did what they could to make the others look good instead of doing stuff to make them look bad.

**117**

So what could she do? It was easy to talk about, but it was hard to figure out what action to take.

Ducky stood up. "I guess I'd better go. I'm glad I came, Sister Truesdale. Thanks for all the advice."

Sister Truesdale stood up too. "Didn't give any. You made all the decisions."

Ducky thought about it, then grinned. "You're pretty sly, aren't you?"

Sister Truesdale grinned back. "How's that?"

"You made me learn something without even realizing it," Ducky said. "What would they say back in Wyoming about that?"

Sister Truesdale didn't even hesitate. "We used to say, 'If you learn a thing a day, you come up smart.'"

Ducky thought about Marybeth and Sunshine and the others as she walked away from Sister Truesdale's house. She thought about them sitting at McDonald's, munching French fries and slurping shakes.

She wished she could be with them.

Well, why couldn't she be?

All she needed to do was walk over to the Golden Arches, go inside, and sit down with them. And say she'd come to help.

Wait a minute. Would Dad say that was being impulsive? Look ahead, she told herself, kicking at a rock on the sidewalk like Jamahl was always doing. What would be the consequences?

They might say they were having a private meeting and she should bug off.

Or they might say, "Sit down, Ducky. We're glad you came."

She would take the chance.

"Sit down, Ducky," Elena said when Ducky showed up at McDonald's. "We're glad you came."

"We weren't sure you'd want to come with us," Carlie said.

"We thought maybe you'd rather stay with Paula," Becca said.

Becca was the blunt one. She usually said what she was thinking.

"You thought I'd rather be with Paula?" Ducky could hear her voice going up the scale. "With *Paula?*"

The Bee Theres all looked a little sheepish as they nodded.

"You two seem to be together a lot lately," Sunshine said. "She's real smart. We thought you might be bored with us, after her."

"You're both firecrackers," Becca blurted. "You could go anywhere you want with her."

Ducky pulled her chair closer and leaned forward. "Look," she said, "Paula is my campaign manager. I didn't ask her. She asked me." She was going to say she wasn't to blame for everything Paula did, but she decided that sounded wimpy, as if she was backing away from the responsibility of what went on in her own campaign. "I have to work with her, but I'd lots rather be with you." She looked around the circle, at each face. "I miss you, you guys."

Hands reached out. "We miss you too, Ducky," everyone said.

Carlie even wiped a tear from the corner of her eye.

Ducky felt like crying too. Her friends were so beautiful. They'd really brighten up the commercial on Saturday. The thought came to her that instead of having just herself dressed up in an ethnic costume, maybe *all* the Bee Theres could be costumed, representing a *lot* of nationalities, just like Marybeth was suggesting for her campaign platform. Wasn't the voice-over already going to say that people everywhere loved the sports shoe that was being advertised?

Maybe she could suggest that Gruff be in the commercial too. Syd liked spontaneity, and you could certainly expect that from Gruff!

She could talk to Syd about it all, if he called, or at least mention it to Stormi who would pass it along to Syd. Becca could be in a German costume, and

Marybeth in an English one. Why not an English *queen* costume? Sure! Then Ducky could get some stills of Marybeth looking like a queen and hang them around the campus on Monday before everyone voted that afternoon.

That would help her, wouldn't it?

She'd better not mention the costumes to the Bee Theres yet, but now was definitely the time to talk about being in the commercial.

She looked at the other girls. "You know what? I'm going to be shooting a commercial on Saturday, and you can all be in it too, if you want to."

Their faces brightened, but they looked puzzled.

"Be in a commercial?" Sunshine said. "On TV?"

"Yes," Ducky said. "Will you do it?"

Marybeth grinned at the others. "Will we do it?"

"Whoo, whoo, whoo," they all said, cranking their arms in the air.

"What do we have to do?" Becca asked excitedly.

Ducky tried to look mysterious. "Wait and see. Maybe just be in the background, but maybe more."

Maybe Syd wouldn't go for having them all costumed. But would it hurt to ask? "Qué será, será" was fine, but why not try to nudge "what will be" in a certain direction?

She just hoped it wouldn't be another great big disaster.

121

# CHAPTER
## 13

As Ducky expected, her dad was upset about the goat being brought on campus. But it wasn't a yell-and-holler upset. It was more a deep-sigh-and-what-will-you-do-next type of thing.

He didn't even remind her that she'd been impulsive again.

She didn't use the excuse that she had brought Gruff only to the edge of the campus, and that it was Paula who had actually yanked him across the lawn and onto the platform.

"I guess it wouldn't do any good to make you promise that you won't do such a thing again," her dad said. He was putting together a macaroni casserole in the kitchen, which probably meant that Mom would be late getting home from work.

"No, sir." This was another of those times when

Dad was the Voice of Authority. "You know how I am, sir."

Ducky thought about the idea she'd had back at McDonald's. "In fact, sir, I'd like to request permission to take the goat on campus Saturday when we're shooting a shoe commercial." She hadn't checked it out with Syd yet, but she might as well get clearance.

Dad's eyebrows went up. "A goat in a shoe commercial?"

He didn't flat out say no. "Well, see," Ducky hurried to say while he was in a lenient mood, "I haven't checked with Stormi yet to make sure they want him, but if they do it'll make a terrific commercial with the Bee Theres and all of us dressed in ethnic clothes like Marybeth says we should do to get to know each other better and Gruff will be part of it."

Ducky knew that what she'd just said didn't make one ounce of sense to her dad.

His eyes looked a little glassy when she finished. He put up a hand. "Ducky, don't ask. Like they say, 'It's easier to get forgiveness than permission.' So go ahead and do what you're going to do anyway, as long as it doesn't hurt anybody and doesn't violate too many laws." He finished grating some cheese and sprinkled it on top of his casserole, then bent over to put the whole thing in the oven.

Straightening up, he said, "I'm glad Anton and

Dermott aren't around to hear me say that." He grinned at Ducky.

She grinned back. "Where are Anton and Dermott, anyway?"

Dad handed her a dishcloth, which meant she should clean up the mess he'd made fixing the casserole. "Don't know. They said they had something to do on campus."

"Which campus? The high school? Franklin Elementary?" She suspected it was neither of them. "Or the junior high? Is Jamahl with them?"

"Don't know. Didn't ask. Hope not to have to find out." Dad picked up the *Los Angeles Times* from the table and headed for his den to read it.

"Daddy?" Ducky said to his back.

He looked over his shoulder.

"I love you," she said.

She felt shy about saying it.

"I love you too, honey," her dad said. "And if we all stick together, we'll all make it through."

Ducky puzzled over that one as she headed for the telephone to see if Stormi was still at her office.

She punched in Stormi's number and waited for the phone to ring. Once, twice, three times. After the fourth ring, Stormi's answering machine came on. "This is Stormi," it said, "and I hope your life is full of rainbows. Please leave your name and number and I'll call you back if it doesn't rain."

It was always fun to hear what Stormi's machine would say. She changed it almost every day.

After the beep, Ducky left a message for Stormi to call her as soon as possible.

She cleaned up the kitchen, then went to her room to write in her diary and study. It wouldn't do to flunk just because she was running for president of the seventh grade.

As she sat down, she looked at the poster of the back of a girl's head. "How did *your* campaign come out?" she asked.

Mom, Anton, and Dermott came home within minutes of one another. Dad whipped his macaroni casserole out of the oven while Ducky tore lettuce and cut tomatoes for a salad.

Ducky waited until they were all seated around the kitchen table before she asked Anton and Dermott where they'd been.

"Guy business," Anton said.

"Yeah," said Dermott. "Guys."

They were so smug.

"You were at the junior high," Ducky said.

Anton put on a surprised look. "Were we?"

"Were we?" echoed Dermott.

Ducky tried again. "Was Jamahl with you?"

"Jamahl who?" Anton said with an innocent look.

Dermott giggled. "What Jamahl?"

Ducky decided she wasn't going to get anywhere that way. She cleared her throat. "I really appreciate the effort you've been putting in to trash my campaign," she said. "I was just wondering what I can expect tomorrow."

"Sunshine and smog," Anton said. "I believe that's what the weather report said."

"Sunshine and smog," Dermott repeated. They exchanged a high five.

Ducky opened her mouth to yell at them, but before she said anything she caught Dad's eye.

He winked. "Don't ask," the wink seemed to say.

She should be grateful they cared enough about her to trash her when she asked them to.

But they didn't need to be so majorly gleeful about it.

"Mom," she said, "how was *your* day?"

Ducky found out soon enough what Anton and Dermott had been up to. The next morning, right after the homeroom repetition of the Pledge of Allegiance, the intercom system began quacking. After a few quacks there were yells of, "We want Ducky, we want Ducky," then more quacking.

Ms. Larsen, Ducky's English teacher, looked annoyed as she glared up at the intercom.

"How long is this going to go on, Ducky?" she asked.

"I don't know," Ducky admitted. She was going to say that her brother and cousin had set it up and she didn't know how long they'd made it. But then it occurred to her that she'd given the quacking tape to Paula.

So Paula was doing this.

Well, good. It *was* annoying, all those ear-bashing quacks while the teachers were trying to get their classes going.

So that would be one strike against her.

But the kids in her homeroom liked it. They started quacking along with the tape. They chanted, "We want Ducky, we want Ducky."

Ms. Larsen finally sent Ducky to the office to ask to have the tape shut off.

There were at least a dozen kids already at the office with similar messages from other classrooms. They all quacked and chanted when they saw Ducky.

Dad looked stern when he came out of the office to hear the complaints.

"The message is not originating from this office," he said. "Miss Dumont, will you please find its source and tell whoever is doing it to scrub it?"

At least he didn't seem to be blaming her directly. Maybe he too thought Anton and Dermott had set it up.

Ducky had a pretty good idea of where the message was coming from. The sound room in the auditorium had access to the intercom system.

She found Paula there, running the tape machine.

Paula turned it off willingly enough.

"We got our message across," she said. "We'll play it again for a while this afternoon."

"I'd rather you didn't," Ducky told her. "The teachers hate it."

Paula shrugged. "Let them hate it. The kids love it, and they're the ones who count."

"Please don't play it again." Ducky hated to sound as if she were pleading with Paula.

Paula smiled.

Ducky was sure the tape would be played again.

So if Anton and Dermott hadn't set up the tape, what *had* they done? Noon came, and nothing else happened. Were they just teasing her, letting her be on edge all day waiting for the sky to fall in when they really hadn't done *anything*?

During the noon break, Eddie had his tuba quartet march up and down the quad. They played march music while some of his supporters came behind them pulling a little racing cart on which he was seated.

There were posters on each side of the cart that proclaimed "Vote for Eddie, leading the race."

Chester Burkey had come up with a giant-sized cardboard computer that he and his friends hauled to the center of the quad. There was a big sign on it that said, "Our tomorrows will byte the dust without up-to-date equipment to prepare us. Vote for Chester and computure own future."

Not bad, Ducky decided.

Marybeth's offering was cute. She and the other Bee Theres had made a giant pot out of chicken wire and papier-mâché. A sign on it said, "Woodward Junior High is a stew of many nations. Come as you are on Monday, and let's see all the ingredients."

The Bee Theres stood around the pot, explaining that "come as you are" meant for everyone to come wearing something that indicated the country of their ancestry.

They handed out little paper U.S. flags to symbolize that no matter where the kids or their ancestors came from, they were all Americans.

"Nice," Ducky told them when she got close enough to speak.

Marybeth smiled. "Remember now, you're going to tell us about Kwanzaa."

Ducky nodded. "I remember. And you remember, you're going to come be in my commercial on Saturday."

"We remember," the Bee Theres chorused.

Ducky wondered if Stormi would call after school. If not, it might be too late to suggest her idea about costumes. And Gruff.

"What are you handing out today?" Sunshine asked.

"Wait and see," was all Ducky could say. She had forgotten to ask Paula when she went to the sound room if there would be any handouts. Maybe there wouldn't.

But there were more quacks and chants over the intercom during the first class after lunch break. Ducky was sent again to tell Paula to cool it. She was so upset that she forgot to ask about handouts.

When the intercom began squawking again just before the end of the last period, everybody thought there would be more quacking. Instead, Jamahl's voice came over the system.

"All seventh graders," he said, "please come to the front lawn to get your fortune quackers."

"Fortune quackers?" said someone in Ducky's math class. "What's a fortune quacker?"

The whole class looked at Ducky.

She tried to look as if she knew.

"Go to the front lawn and find out," she said.

The front lawn was crowded when Ducky got there. Jamahl and the other guys from church were handing out little orange paper duck beaks. Jamahl didn't look particularly happy. In fact, his face drooped when he looked at Ducky.

At least she knew now what Anton and Dermott and Jamahl had been doing the afternoon before— making fortune quackers.

Somebody handed one of the "quackers" to Ducky.

On the outside was printed, "Vote for Ducky." Underneath that, it said, "Don't make quacks, just look inside."

Inside was a little slip of paper, like in a fortune cookie.

Ducky's slip said, "If you were twice as smart, you'd still be a half-wit."

A guy was laughing about his fortune. "Listen to this," he said. "'You think you're a big cheese—but you only smell like one.'"

Insults. That's what Anton and Dermott and Jamahl had come up with to trash her. The kids would read them and get mad and not vote for her.

A few of the guys were snickering about their fortunes, the kind of snickering you hear when somebody has said something tasteless.

But mostly, the kids were silent as they read the little slips of paper.

Ducky felt sick. This wasn't the way she'd planned to go down. Not by making kids feel bad.

Somebody whacked Ducky on the back. "I don't know what we did for fun before you came," he said in kind of a sarcastic way.

Suddenly the Bee Theres were there beside her.

"Don't take any," she told them.

But it was too late. Marybeth was pulling a slip from inside an orange "quacker."

"'If you want to lose ten pounds of ugly fat,'" she read, "'just cut off your head.'"

"I'm sorry, Marybeth," Ducky said. "It doesn't mean anything."

Marybeth's mouth twitched as if she were trying to smile. But Ducky knew the insults were too much.

She could see that Jamahl felt bad about it. And she couldn't blame Anton and Dermott. They'd only done what she'd asked them to do.

Once again the blame rested squarely on her.

# CHAPTER
# 14

Kids were turning away from Ducky as if they didn't quite know what to say.

Nobody was going to vote for her now.

Wasn't that what she wanted? Now the kids would vote for Marybeth, and she'd be a terrific president.

Goal achieved.

But Ducky hadn't wanted to go down this way. Hurting people's feelings was not what she wanted to be remembered for. It wasn't what she was or ever would be.

The Bee Theres were still standing beside Ducky. "Did Paula do this?" Becca asked. She sounded as if she would probably go poke Paula in the nose if Ducky said yes.

Ducky shook her head. "No," she said. "She

didn't have anything to do with it. I can't blame anybody but myself."

Becca looked at her for a moment, then hugged her. That was almost worse than if she'd yelled at her.

The simple hug made Ducky want to cry.

Elena was walking toward Jamahl. "I haven't got my quacker yet," she said. "May I please have one?"

For a moment it seemed as if Jamahl wasn't even going to give her one. But then, his face lengthening even more, he handed one to her.

She pulled out the little slip and read, " 'Roses are red, grasses are green, you have a shape like a washing machine.'"

She laughed, then turned to Ducky. "These are funny," she said. "I'm going to gather up a bunch to take home to my brothers. They'll *love* them." She took a whole handful of the quackers from Jamahl, then reached over to take some from Sam.

"I want some too," Carlie said. "My brother really yucks it up over this kind of stuff."

She took all the quackers that Gregory had left.

Ducky knew what they were doing. They were gathering up all the remaining quackers before any more of the kids got them.

Now a lot of the guys were rereading their insults and laughing.

"Hey, Ducky," one guy said, "these are great. You must have stayed up all night to think them up."

Ducky smiled.

Other guys were grabbing any leftover quackers. They were even asking the girls if they could have theirs. Several girls said no, they wanted to keep them.

"My brother's really going to get it tonight," one girl said. "He's always throwing stuff like this at me."

Suddenly it was a contest to see who could gather up the most insults to take home. It seemed as if everybody wanted to use them on their brothers.

Guy stuff. Was this what Anton and Dermott meant when they said they'd been doing guy stuff? Guys seemed to like insulting one another.

Sunshine was yelling something. "Ducky is not responsible for any aftereffects of your fortune quackers," she said. "And don't use them on your parents. That could be really hazardous to your health."

"No way," somebody said. "My ma would fry my hide if I said something like this to her."

There was a lot of laughing as kids headed for home. They smiled at Ducky now, and some of them even thanked her.

She stood with the other Bee Theres until they and Jamahl, Sam, Arvy, and Gregory were the only ones left.

"Thanks, you guys," she said, "for being there. You really saved me."

"Well," Marybeth said, "it certainly wasn't like you."

She seemed a little puzzled.

But Ducky wasn't going to mention that it hadn't been her idea at all.

Jamahl looked as if he might say something. He probably wanted to apologize for what he and Anton and Dermott had done.

But Ducky shook her head just a little. If he said anything about it, the Bee Theres would wonder why Ducky had allowed the guys to do it, and then the whole miserable story about how she was trying to lose the election might come out.

"You know how I get carried away sometimes," Ducky said with a laugh.

The others nodded and laughed along with her.

"Bishop Tolman would say it was a good learning experience," Arvy said.

Ducky remembered what Sister Truesdale had told her. "If you learn a thing a day, you come up smart," she said.

It seemed as if the whole thing had turned out all right. But she was back to square one, wasn't she? She still had to figure out how to make sure she lost the election.

Dermott must have been watching for Ducky to come home, because she heard his microphone squawk as soon as she set foot on the porch.

"Here comes Ducky," Dermott blared over the mike. "Is that really her face, or did her neck throw up? Did you know Ducky went to the zoo yesterday—and was accepted? And have you heard about—"

Abruptly he stopped.

He was yelling as Ducky opened the front door and went into the living room, where Dermott stood by a window. "Who cut off my sound?" he hollered. "Anton, did you shut me down?"

"Yes," Anton said from the family room. "Cool it, Demented."

"How come?" Dermott demanded. He looked over at Ducky. "I was just having fun," he said limply.

Anton came into the living room. He stood there, looking a little sadly at Ducky. "I'm sorry, sis," he said.

Sorry? Anton? Ducky stared at him. Since when had Anton ever been sorry for anything he ever did to her? Did her big brother really, actually, unbelievably have a heart?

"I asked for it," she said. "I asked you to trash me."

Anton shook his head. "Not that way. I got to thinking about it after we did it. You would never do that kind of thing."

Dermott was looking from one to the other.

137

"What's going on?" he asked. "Are you mad at me, Ducky?"

He looked so upset that Ducky knew he was wondering again if he'd get kicked out of their home for bad behavior.

"Dermott," she said, "you're my very favorite cousin. How could I be mad at you?"

Dermott's eyes opened wide with surprise. "Really? Do you really like me, Ducky?"

She went over and put one arm around his neck and scrubbed the knuckles of her other hand across the top of his head, the way Anton did sometimes.

"I really do, you little twerp," she said.

She wondered if anybody had ever "been there" for Dermott the way the Bee Theres and the guys from church had "been there" for her that day.

"I do dumb things," Dermott said.

Ducky nodded. "So do I. Even Anton does."

"Who, me?" Anton said.

They all laughed.

"It's okay, guys," Ducky said. "The kids still like me."

"So what are you going to do now to lose the election?" Dermott asked.

"I'm going to call Stormi," Ducky said.

Leaving Anton and Dermott looking bewildered, she headed for the telephone.

Stormi loved her idea about costuming her friends and using Gruff in the commercial.

"Have you told Syd about it?" she asked.

When Ducky said he hadn't called, Stormi said, "Well, I'll call him right now. He never knows just what he wants to do until the shooting starts anyway. Let me write down your costume suggestions and the girls' sizes."

Ducky named each girl and told Stormi the dress sizes, emphasizing that Marybeth should have a queen costume.

"Not a problem," Stormi said. "The costume department has everything. So be prepared for anything on Saturday. And bring the goat."

Ducky had no sooner hung up the telephone than Paula called.

"You almost blew the whole campaign with those dumb insults," she screeched without even saying hello. "Didn't I tell you to stay out of it until election day?"

Ducky's head was beginning to ache. "Whose campaign is it, anyway?" She was surprised at herself for talking back to Paula.

Wasn't she afraid of her anymore? No, she wasn't, she decided. She wasn't going to let Paula jerk her strings anymore.

"It *was* a dumb idea," she admitted. "But if I *want*

139

to use dumb ideas in my own campaign, then I'll *use* dumb ideas, Paula."

There was a moment of silence.

Ducky swallowed nervously. Would Paula's reaction explode her eardrum? She held the telephone a couple of inches from her head, just in case.

"Okay, Ducky." Paula's voice was as smooth and dry as chalk dust. "It's just that you're such a strong candidate who could really throw a lot of weight around. This is such a great chance that I'd hate to fluff it."

Her voice lowered as if she were telling secrets. "Ducky, if we get into power this year, we can rule the school until we graduate and maybe even take over the high school."

She sounded like one of those dictators Mr. Sorensen talked about in social studies class. "Today the seventh grade, tomorrow the world!"

"Frankly, Paula," Ducky said, "I don't want to rule the school. In fact . . ."

Paula waited, then asked, "In fact what?"

Ducky had been going to say right out that she didn't even want to win this election. But she wouldn't put it past Paula to figure out why and announce it around so that Marybeth and everybody else would know. So she just said, "In fact, right now I'm not looking beyond tomorrow."

"That's what I was really calling about." Paula's voice was brisk now. "There won't be a lot going on tomorrow or Friday, but on Monday I want Gruff at school again. Everybody loves him, and the goat vote will be high. So I want you to arrange for him to be there while the voting is going on. Kind of as a reminder, you know."

"It's against the rules to bring animals on campus," Ducky protested.

"What do we care about rules?" Paula purred. "He's been there before, and he can be there again. So bring him. I'll do anything to win."

It really wasn't any use to protest, Ducky decided. She'd be taking Gruff on campus Saturday for the commercial, so on Monday she'd only be breaking again an already broken rule.

And if things worked out the way she hoped, it might just be a great benefit to Marybeth to have Gruff on campus.

"Okay, Paula," she said. "I'll do whatever you want."

# CHAPTER
15

Friday morning dragged by. Ducky could barely concentrate on any of her classes. Her thoughts seemed to be on a playback tape that echoed Paula's words over and over again: "Goat vote, vote, vote, vote, vote. What do we care about the rules? Anything to win, win, win, win, win."

Just before the lunch break she got a message to come to the principal's office.

What had she done wrong? On the way to the office, she thought back over possible misdeeds. She couldn't remember any that hadn't been patched up. She hoped there weren't any new ones. She knew she'd about used up her quota in her dad's eyes.

On the way down the corridor she met Jamahl. He looked troubled as he came over to walk beside her.

"Ducky," he said. "I've got something to say."

He glanced at her, then looked shyly at the floor. They walked a little way in silence.

"So say it," Ducky prompted.

Jamahl cleared his throat. "You know that old story about King Midas? Did you read that in elementary?"

"Sure," Ducky said. "Everything he touched turned to gold."

"Well," Jamahl said, "I think you have the golden touch. Everything you touch turns out okay, even when we try to make you look bad." He still had his head down, but he gave her another shy glance through his eyelashes. "I don't want to try to trash you anymore, Ducky." He shook his head as if to emphasize what he said.

"You don't have to trash me anymore," she said. "I've decided that whatever will be, will be."

Jamahl looked relieved. "Qué será, será," he said.

Ducky was surprised. "Jamahl, I didn't know you knew Spanish."

He nodded. "I lived in Mexico for a while. One of my grandmas is Mexican."

Ducky didn't know that about Jamahl, either.

There were a lot of things she didn't know about Jamahl. But there was one thing she did know. Jamahl liked her.

He raised his head. Looking straight at her, he said, "I just wanted you to know. I think you'd be a terrific president, Ducky."

He hurried away.

Ducky watched him go. There was another thing she knew. She liked Jamahl.

It made her want to skip the rest of the way down the hall, but she didn't do it. People didn't generally skip in junior high. It wasn't cool.

When she got to the principal's office, Ducky found that her summons was nothing to worry about. It was just a message from Syd, the director of the shoe commercial, telling her that yes, he liked her idea as Stormi had explained it to him. He would costume her friends and maybe even use the goat. This could be one of his best commercials, he said. In addition, he said, he had decided he could use a lot of kids as background because he wanted it to look like an ordinary school day. He said he would arrange for a $10 per person donation to the school, and asked if she could round up the kids.

Ducky was dismayed about Syd wanting more kids. She had planned this to be something really special and different for the Bee Theres. Then she would arrange to get the stills of Marybeth in her queen costume to hang around the campus on Monday, the day of the voting.

The way she'd planned it, this would focus a whole lot of attention on Marybeth. It might ruin everything to have *everybody* there at the shoot.

But how could she not do what Syd wanted? He was the boss.

So, after getting official permission from her dad, Ducky wrote up an announcement to go out over the intercom system.

The whole school buzzed about it the rest of the day. It looked as if Syd would be getting all the kids he needed.

On Saturday morning Ducky went to Sister Truesdale's house to pick up Gruff. Sister Truesdale was going to trust her to be in charge of him; she didn't want to wait around during the whole shooting process.

Ducky told her about the new development. "Maybe I shouldn't have messed around with the commercial in the first place," she said. "Marybeth's going to get lost in the crowd, with everybody there. The other candidates will probably come too." She sighed. "I wish I'd never gotten involved in this election thing. I wish—"

Sister Truesdale interrupted. "Back in Wyoming we used to say that a wishbone is no substitute for a backbone. So let's just get on with it. When the horse is gone, it's too late to lock the barn door."

She got Gruff's lead and fastened it to his collar, then handed it to Ducky.

"To tell the truth," she said, "this may work out just fine. Everybody will see Marybeth in her queen costume. If she's as impressive as you think she's going to be, it will be better than just a picture to hang up on Monday."

That made Ducky a little happier as she and Gruff started for the campus.

Gruff was excited about going somewhere again. He tossed his head and nibbled at Ducky's jeans and bleated at passersby.

People waved at him from cars, and little kids yelled to ask where he was going.

As always, Gruff was very popular.

If only the goat vote could be channeled in Marybeth's direction, she'd be sure to win.


Even though it was quite a while before the shoot was to start, there were hundreds of kids already gathered on the campus when Ducky and Gruff got there. It looked as if all Woodward Junior High's students had come and brought their friends as well.

Eddie had apparently decided to use the opportunity for a little more campaigning. He was there with his VOTE FOR EDDIE signs and his tuba quartet, which was making oompah music that some of the kids were dancing to.

Paula wore her Power Ranger costume and carried a sign that said, "RULE THE SCHOOL. VOTE FOR DUCKY."

Ducky wondered if she should tell Eddie and Paula to ditch the signs. But she knew that Syd was very creative as well as spontaneous. He might want to use them. She would leave it up to him.

A lot of kids cheered when they saw Ducky, but the cheers may have been for Gruff. He nodded his head as if acknowledging his fans, and they cheered some more, crowding around to pat him.

Ducky, with Gruff trying to hang back with his admirers, went straight to the trailer that was the director's traveling office.

Syd leaped to his feet when Ducky stuck her head through the door. "What'd you do?" he yelped. "Invite every kid in the state of California to come?" He tore at his hair, a sure sign that he was upset. "We expected fifty, maybe seventy-five kids. We got an army. Ten bucks a head—you trying to break us or something? We can't work with this mob."

Uh-oh. Was her whole plan going to collapse? Where was her Midas touch when she needed it?

Ducky cleared her throat. She knew Syd pretty well after having worked with him on several shoots.

"This mob will probably all buy the shoes you're advertising," Ducky said. "The sponsor will be happy."

Syd stopped tearing his hair and looked at her.

"Besides," she continued, "you'll figure out how to use everybody. You're such a genius, Syd."

He nodded. "*That's* true." He gazed out at the crowd.

"Take your friends to the costume truck," he said briskly. "Let's get started."

It was only then that he noticed Gruff had been sampling a stack of papers on a little folding table just outside the door.

"My script," Syd hollered. "This monster is digesting my script!" Snatching Gruff's snack just before it disappeared down his throat, he held it up. "Call the police! Get this beast out of here!" He tore at his hair again.

People scurried around, punching buttons on cellular phones and flapping arms at Gruff.

Ducky stood on the little steps of the trailer. "No," she shouted. "It's okay. Gruff is part of the commercial."

She turned to Syd. As soothingly as she could, she said, "Remember what a good idea you had about using the goat?" Actually, it had been *her* idea, but it seemed best to forget that at the moment. "Remember how you said this could be one of your best commercials?"

The big crowd of kids watched as she calmed Syd down. They'd be impressed by the way she handled the situation. They'd vote for her.

Oh well. Qué será, será. She'd be a good president, and then she and the other Bee Theres could lay the groundwork for Marybeth to run for *eighth*-grade class president next year.

Syd simmered down enough to smile and pat Gruff gingerly on the head. "That's *right*," he said. "The goat. We've got shoes for him." Turning back to Ducky, he said, "Send him off with Annabelle, and you and your friends go get dressed. What are you waiting for, Christmas?"

Ducky felt limp with relief. She handed Gruff's leash to the girl named Annabelle. Locating the other Bee Theres, she beckoned them to follow her.

They were excited about being there in the midst of all the cameras and trucks and people. And all of them were happy about the clothes the costume trailer provided for them. Elena got a red, full-skirted Mexican dress that brought out all her vivid good looks. Becca's costume was a German dirndl that nipped in her waist and made her look as if she had bosoms, which thrilled her. Carlie looked exotic in her Japanese kimono with her hair piled on top of her head and stuck through with a couple of spikes that looked like knitting needles.

Ducky was given a flowing African robe with bright orange, brown, yellow, and green stripes. The costume lady tied a bright orange scarf around her head, draping it so that even Ducky had to admit she looked great. Sunshine was in a fantastic American colonial costume. And Marybeth looked best of all in a glittering medieval royal gown of a rich burgundy color with huge sleeves and a train. She wore a crown that glittered as if it were made of real diamonds.

Marybeth stood very straight, with her head held high. Anybody could see she was capable of running a country, to say nothing of Woodward Junior High.

On their feet all of the girls wore the sports shoes the commercial was featuring. The shoes looked out of place with the fancy costumes, but the voice-overs that would be added later would take care of that. They'd say something about everybody, absolutely everybody, no matter who they were or where they came from, preferring that brand of sports shoes.

The Bee Theres attracted a lot of attention when they came out of the costume trailer. Somebody yelled to Marybeth, "Hey, Queenie, you can rule my school any day."

Annabelle led Gruff up to the trailer. He pranced

along with tiny sports shoes, created especially for him, fastened on each of his four hooves.

He gave Ducky a glance, but apparently decided he was now too exalted to associate with anything less than royalty, because he went straight over to Marybeth. Gazing at her with adoring eyes, he nibbled at the velvet trimming on her dress. His little beard—which still held a few flecks of Syd's script—quivered, and his stubby tail flicked back and forth like a dog's.

Marybeth watched him with delight. "Sir Goat," she said. "I dub you my Knight of Honor."

Syd liked it. "Catch that," he yelled to a cameraman. "Focus on the shoes."

Using a bullhorn, he yelled for the kids to act as if they were just coming to school. He positioned the Bee Theres here and there in the crowd, directing the cameramen to pick them out. "Focus on the shoes," he said again.

Syd also liked the signs that Eddie and Paula had brought. He told the cameramen to be sure to include them.

Paula must have thought that entitled her to be the center of attention, because she tried to push Gruff aside so she could get closer to a camera.

Gruff detached himself from Marybeth's dress and bleated a protest.

Paula whapped him on the rear with her sign.

Gruff didn't take kindly to being whapped. He turned to glare at Paula. His legs stiffened, and his head swung from side to side.

Ducky began to worry. Did he remember the day Paula had dragged him up on the platform at school?

"Ba-a-a-a-a-AH!" Gruff said.

"Get out of my way, you smelly wretch," Paula snarled. She bashed him with the sign again, just as Eddie's tuba quartet let go with a loud oompah.

Startled, Gruff danced toward Paula, his head lowered.

"Help!" she screeched. "That beast is going to butt me! Help!"

Security people yanked walkie-talkies from their pockets. "Goat alert," one of them yelled. "We need help in here."

Marybeth tugged at Gruff's little stub of a tail, trying to hold him back. "He won't hurt anybody," she said. "He's just scared."

Paula screeched louder.

Gruff snorted at her.

Kids laughed and hooted.

Gruff continued to make little darting motions toward Paula, whose shrieks ripped through people's ears.

Ducky tried to move forward to stand by Gruff,

but there were too many kids in the way. A security guy shoved through, a billy club in his hand.

He must have spotted the flecks of white in Gruff's beard because he held his walkie-talkie to his mouth and yelled, "Berserk goat. Maybe rabid. Need backup."

"Cut," Syd yelled over the bullhorn. "Cut."

As far as Ducky could see, the cameras continued to roll.

"Stand back, everybody," the security guy shouted, brandishing his billy club. "I'll drop him."

Marybeth moved in front of Gruff, holding out her full skirt to protect him. "You'll have to drop *me* before you touch a hair of his head," she yelled.

"Attagirl," Ducky whispered silently.

Kids cheered.

The tuba quartet oompahed.

"Cut! Cut! Cut! Cut!" Syd wailed hopelessly.

The cameras rolled on.

It all ended with Marybeth, in her queenly robes with her sports shoes braced firmly against the school steps, clutching Gruff tightly around the neck while she yelled defiance at the security men and Gruff chewed serenely on one of her shoes.

Paula was furious, and so was Syd.

"Ducky Dumont," he yelled into the bullhorn. "This is all your fault. That goat was *your* idea. Forget about this commercial, and forget about working with me ever again."

Paula threw down her sign. "That goes for me too," she said stomping away. "I'm finished with you."

But as Ducky watched the kids push up to talk to Marybeth, she decided there was both bad news and good news to write about in her diary.

The bad news was that she'd ruined her chances to do any more commercials.

The good news was that there was plenty of attention focused on Marybeth. She'd get the goat vote, all right.

So the Midas touch was still operating. But it sure could be tricky sometimes.

# CHAPTER
# 16

Ducky didn't sleep well that night. When she finally did drift off, she had a nice dream about Marybeth being queen of the Tournament of Roses Parade and riding high on a float with Gruff beside her. As the float moved along Colorado Boulevard, Gruff shook his little beard at the crowd and said, "Ba-a-a-a-a-ah!"

It was a funny dream and Ducky was giggling when Dermott awakened her with a blast from his microphone.

"Telephone for Ducky," he announced. "Get out of bed, Ducky, and come to the phone."

It all came back to her then. She had ruined her chances to do more commercials. But at least Marybeth was going to be president.

She peered at her alarm clock as she slid out of

bed. It was almost 9:30. She hadn't slept that late in a long time.

Padding out into the hall, she grabbed the upstairs extension. It must be one of the Bee Theres calling. Maybe they were going to have an emergency meeting that day. She was glad they were including her.

"Hello?" she said, hoping her voice didn't sound as if she'd just gotten up.

"Ducky dearie," a male voice said in her ear. "Syd here. You'll never believe the fabulous film footage we got yesterday."

Fabulous? What was he talking about? He'd fired her, hadn't he? Everything had been a fiasco.

"Really?" she said.

"Really," Syd said. "We'll have to do a lot of cutting and splicing and editing, and we'll have to rewrite the voice-over material. But I'm telling you, my idea to have that goat in the commercial was in*spired*. And the way I got him to chew on that shoe at the end? Well, my dearie, this is going to be my best work ever."

Ducky didn't bother to remind him that yesterday he'd been only too happy to blame the goat idea on her, and that chewing up the shoe had been Gruff's idea, not Syd's. All she said was, "That's great, Syd."

So why had he called?

He told her. "Ducky dearie," he said, "I want you and those dear little friends of yours to be in a follow-up commercial. And that *mar*velous goat, of course. I think we have a new star on our hands."

"You're a genius, Syd," Ducky said.

"*That's* true," Syd said. "Ta-ta, Ducky dearie." He hung up.

Ducky could hardly wait to call the other Bee Theres. "Come over to my house," she told each one. "I have something to tell you."

She got dressed and went downstairs, where she found her dad and mom and Anton preparing to go somewhere.

"We didn't wake you for breakfast," Mom said. "You seemed to need the sleep."

Dad rolled his eyes, but he didn't say anything about yesterday's events.

Ducky had told her family all about the goat adventure, of course. Now she told them the good news about how the whole thing had turned out to be a success.

Dad grinned. "You have a real talent for landing on your feet, Ducky," he said.

That was a lot like Jamahl's saying she had the Midas touch.

Mom and Anton and Dermott were generous with compliments too, which made Ducky feel so good that she agreed to be in charge of Dermott while the others were gone.

Dermott settled down in his room with his mike. The Bee Theres hadn't come yet, so Ducky went to her own room to catch up on her diary. After getting it out from the hidden space behind the little door in her closet, she wrote all the good and bad news from yesterday and today.

She wrote until Dermott announced over his mike that Becca, Carlie, Elena, Marybeth, and Sunshine were getting out of Becca's mom's car in front of the house.

Leaving her diary on her dressing table, Ducky ran downstairs.

"I'm so glad you could all come," she said, flinging the door open for her friends. Waving good-bye to Becca's mom, she said, "Wait till I tell you!"

They all came in rather cautiously, their eyes questioning.

"Is it about yesterday?" Becca asked. "Did you get into more trouble with your commercials people?"

"I'm sorry about that," Marybeth said. "It was all my fault. But I couldn't let those security guys hurt Gruff."

"No, no," Ducky said, motioning for them all to sit around the kitchen table. "It's *good* news, you guys. Really good."

They turned their faces toward her.

"How would you all like to be in *another* commercial?" she asked.

They all squealed with delight.

Ducky told them all about what Syd had said. She was in the middle of saying, "And he wants Gruff, too," when she heard Dermott's mike squawk upstairs.

" 'Paula says I'm a sure winner,'" Dermott began. " 'I'd kind of like to be president, but the trouble is, Marybeth really wants the job. She'd probably hate me if I won, and so would the other Bee Theres.'"

Ducky listened in horror. Dermott was reading her diary!

"Dermott!" she hollered, pushing her chair back and starting for the stairs.

But it was too late.

" 'I'd rather be one of the Bee Theres than be president of anything,'" Dermott went on at high volume. " 'So I've got to figure out some way to make sure I lose.'"

Ducky was upstairs now. Hurtling into her room, she snatched the diary away from Dermott, then grabbed his mike and switched it off.

"Hey," he said, "I was just getting to the best part, where we try to trash you."

"Dermott." She made an effort to keep her voice

from being a roar. "Didn't anybody ever tell you it's a serious crime to read another person's diary?"

His eyes got big. "I was just reading the parts I thought those other girls would be interested in. Was that bad?"

"Yes," she said. But then she softened because he got that familiar look on his face, the one that said he was worried that he might get kicked out of their home.

She remembered what she'd realized a couple days ago, that Dermott had never had anybody who was there for him. Maybe she should be turning her Midas touch his way so that everything would come out all right for him.

But she was still mad at him.

"Dermott," she said, "you're a great kid. I really like you. *But . . .* "

He looked a little relieved. "*But* I did something wrong, didn't I?"

"A whopper," she said. "You should *never* look inside another person's diary without permission, much less announce it to the whole world."

"I'm sorry, Ducky," he said.

She could tell that he really was sorry. "I know. And that's why I'm forgiving you." To show she meant it, she knuckled the top of his head. "But you know what? My friends didn't know I was trying to lose the election. I don't know how they're going to take it."

Dermott picked up his mike. "I'll fix it," he said. "I'll tell them I was making it all up. I'll say it was a joke."

Ducky shook her head. "No, we can't say things that aren't true."

She thought about that for a minute. She hadn't exactly been a model of truthfulness the past week. Not that she'd *said* things that weren't true, but certainly her actions hadn't been totally truthful, the way she'd tried to pretend she was running for president while all the time she was trying to lose.

Maybe it was time to confess the whole thing. If she had faced it straight on, the way Sister Truesdale had said, she wouldn't be in this muddle now.

"Dermott," she said. "It's all right. We all make mistakes."

"Not just me?" he said.

"All of us," Ducky assured him. "But if we all hang together we can work things out."

Wasn't that what Dad had said?

Dermott squirmed as she hugged him, but as she headed for the door he said, "Ducky."

She turned back.

"I love you," he said, then hid his head behind his arm as if he were embarrassed.

"I love you too, Demented," she said.

To show she trusted him, she laid her diary down on the chest of drawers by the door before she went downstairs.

The Bee Theres watched her quietly as she came back into the kitchen.

Marybeth was the first to speak. "You were trying to *lose?*" she said. "Why didn't you tell us?"

Ducky took a deep breath. "The truth," she told herself silently.

Aloud, she said, "I didn't tell you because I thought you'd be offended that I was so sure I was going to win that I had to try to lose."

Did that make sense?

Marybeth, Becca, Carlie, Sunshine, and Elena looked at one another. Were they all going to stand up and stomp out of the room, leaving her alone? Were they right then and there going to declare that she was no longer a Bee There?

What they did was burst into laughter.

"Ducky, you goof," Elena said. "You were deliberately trying to make yourself look bad so that people wouldn't vote for you?"

Ducky nodded.

Elena grinned at the other girls. "That explains a lot of things."

Sunshine was grinning too. "You were doing that

while we were running around assuring people they should vote for you because you weren't really Paula's puppet, the way it looked sometimes."

"Huh?" Ducky said. That was about all she could manage.

Carlie spoke next. "Most of the kids know Paula, and they know how she'd be trying to pull your strings if you became president. So we were worried that probably they wouldn't vote for you. But we knew you'd be a terrific president, so we were telling kids to see you for yourself."

Now Ducky had to laugh too. "And I didn't even *want* to be president. I'm voting for Marybeth."

"Thanks," Marybeth said. "But it's okay if I don't win. My ambition is to be president *someday*. If I lose this year, I'll run for eighth-grade president, or ninth-grade."

"Or student body prez in high school," Elena said. "Or the first woman president of the United States."

"You're already a president, Marybeth," Ducky said. "Beehive class president."

Marybeth grinned. "You're right. So what am I worried about? I've just learned that no matter what happens Monday, I've already reached my dream."

Ducky thought about what Sister Truesdale had said.

"Back in Wyoming," she told the Bee Theres,

"they say that if you learn a thing a day, you come up smart. I guess I've learned not to go into things backwards."

She thought of the old campaign poster that had started her off on the wrong path in the first place, the poster that showed only the back of a girl's head. "Wait a minute," she said, running up the stairs to her room.

Her diary was still safe on her dresser. So Dermott had learned a thing that day too.

Grabbing the poster, she ran downstairs and showed it to the other girls. "This is where I got my idea for doing weird stuff," she said.

They examined the poster with interest, commenting on the fifties hairstyle.

"She must have had a lot of confidence," Carlie said, "not to even put her name on it."

Sunshine ran her finger across the short-cropped hair. "I wonder who she was," she mused.

"Let's find out," Becca said. "We'll make it a Bee Theres detective project."

Marybeth was looking at the poster thoughtfully. "I wonder if she was elected president."

"I don't know," Ducky said, "but I don't have to be much of a detective to know that *you're* going to be elected president. After what happened yesterday, you've definitely got the goat vote."

*     *     *

But she was wrong. Marybeth came in second. Or actually third.

Ducky came in fourth.

Eddie was last.

Paula was nowhere.

It was Gruff who got the goat vote and the most votes. A line on the ballot was reserved for write-ins, and a lot of kids who normally would have voted for Ducky or Marybeth wrote in Gruff's name instead, electing him president.

When the Bee Theres went to Sister Truesdale's house to tell him, his only comment was, "Ba-a-a-a-a-ah."

"That means he declines the honor," Sister Truesdale said as fickle Gruff nibbled lovingly at Marybeth's shirttail.

The more serious seventh graders cast their votes for Chester Burkey, so he came in second behind Gruff and was declared president. Most kids were satisfied; they all agreed that the school needed new computers and other equipment.

Jamahl told Ducky he was sorry neither she nor Marybeth had won, but that Chester was a good choice. "He's like a bulldog," Jamahl said. "Kids think he's a nerd, but when he sinks his teeth into something he doesn't let go until people pay attention to him."

Marybeth was declared vice president.

"You would have won," Ducky told her, "if I had never gotten Gruff involved."

"We'll never know," Marybeth said. "It doesn't matter."

"We can start right away planning the next campaign," Ducky said. "This time the Bee Theres will *all* be there for you, Marybeth."

"Unless *you* want to run again," Marybeth said with a grin.

Ducky's only comment was, "Ba-a-a-a-a-ah!"